Three x the Fun

A Rebellion LIT Anthology

Rebellion LIT

Contents

Cover Design by Tiffany Christina Lewis
Title Card Illustrations by Victoria Aden

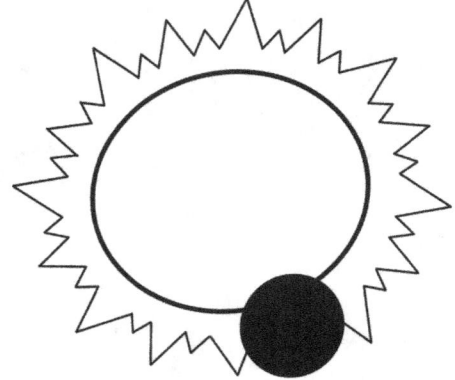

THE SUN SUCKERS
by Noah Browning

The Sun Suckers

By Noah Browning

Some things will always have some form of metaphysical power over others. Death, Love, and Time are examples of this. Yet, one odd case of this is the concept of Currency. It's made up via the culture that made it. Why does it have power? Because the culture says so.

For those who'd say that money isn't needed in our hyper-evolved future, you may not want to read the rest of this. It'd be awful to pop that optimistic bubble formed over your mind.

In the far far future, money has its strongest stranglehold over the universe. People fight desperately for resources, well, people working for corporations. The non-corporate-aligned folk try to live peacefully in their own little pockets of space (usually unsuccessfully).

One popular racket is Sun Forming, the biggest in this business being SunCore Industries. They've produced over ten billion stars over the universe, most aren't even aware they live near a crafted star.

This is where we find Frendrick. Well, more accurately, his name is Frendrick Daev Q'ohQ'oh Puhfs XVII. But, Frendrick works best for him.

It was another average day for him on the ranch. He walked out to see the blazing blue stars outside. He stepped out onto the small world he lived on. He took his daily morning walk around the rock, which only took about ten minutes. He examined the Screw Berries. They were very popular with those into hallucinogens.

One reason was because they were able to make you hallucinate other timelines, the other was that they tasted very good. Their flavor was almost indistinguishable from raspberries. Most eat them unaware of what they are, which usually ends with the person digesting the berry to ask everyone if they're still themselves for days after the fact.

He sat in a rocking chair, drinking out of an almost comically small cup of coffee. He basked in the blue sunlight. He cracked his back in the chair and leaned back. To him this was perfection.

He stared up into the starry sky. He knew this sky like the back of his hand, yet, that large black dot was new. It moved closer and closer to the sun. Now, maybe he was crazy, but he swore he saw something like a large vacuum cleaner pop out of the black dot. In a matter of seconds, the sun was cartoonishly sucked into this small black dot.

Frendrick sat slacked jawed. The black dot got closer and closer until it revealed itself to be ship with a yellowish off-white paint job. A white hazmat-like suit walked out and pointed at Frendrick.

"Are you living on this moon?" the suit asked.

Frendrick only nodded.

"You do know that you were orbiting a SunCore star illegally, right?" the suit said. "You're lucky this wasn't a generational farm or something, that would've been bad for your descendants."

The person in the hazmat suit then hoisted up their pants and gave a small salute to Frendrick.

"Welp, have a good existence. You owe about ten million to SunCore, and have about six half rotations to pay that."

They then proceeded to walk back into their ship and blast off. A packet of paper was launched out the back of the ship and landed in front of Frendrick.

It was a thick packet with a large SunCorp logo on the first page. He leaned over and grabbed it. Though, it was hard to read the packet without a sun.

* * *

Noah Browning is many things: a writer, Filmmaker, an Overthinker, and an overall creative. Heavily influenced by various science fiction and fantasy authors such as Douglas Adams, Neal Stephenson, Terry Pratchett, and Michael

Crichton. He is Florida-born but raised by New Jersey natives, thus he grew up with an interesting clashing of cultures and values. Born Physically disabled, he spent most of his time interacting with various forms of artistic media. Growing up with an overdeveloped sense of media literacy, he strives to one day make his impact with a piece of his own.

The Eternal Mage

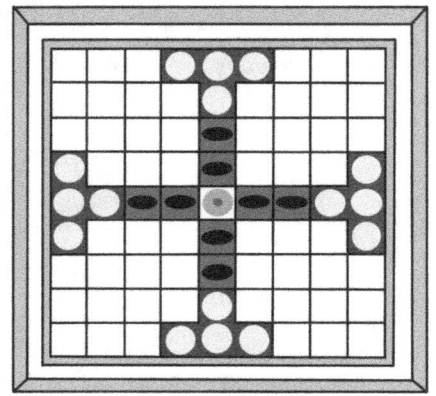

by Joseph S Samaniego

The Eternal Mage

By Joseph S. Samaniego

A melancholic bell rang throughout the stone halls of an ancient temple. A haunting tone that echoed a sense of an old world long forgotten. Life away from any authentic form of society was lonely. That's what Jyrl wanted.

His mind was too stressed, and that was probably an understatement. He, Jyrl, was a talented and respected mage. At least, he used to be. He was intelligent and had been known as a charismatic person once. That was a lifetime ago, or felt like it to the forty-two-year-old mage.

Maybe that was part of the problem.

Expectations of his intelligence, of his talent, it all wrecked and ruined him mentally. What was Jyrl to do? In all corners, he was looked to for guidance and used in this way and that. He had been a leader, an up-and-coming mind and body that had all the potential in the world. People within powerful positions had pegged Jyrl for lofty offices and titles. Jyrl had sought those titles actively. His ambition had pushed him.

And then, as it happens in the world of comeuppance, the potential was wasted, the ambitions were torn asunder, and the loftiness crashed to the ground. All seemingly in one fell swoop. The highly gifted often succumbed to their own mental weariness.

Weariness. That's a nice word for it.

In just eight short years, Jyrl had been nearing the pinnacle of success within his order, just one or two years away from the ruling council. He had an income that afforded him a grandiose life, and his influence was highly sought after. But then, something within Jyrl's mind stopped working as it had been.

His family was unable to help him, and slowly they left. They couldn't take being around his mental anguish and pain. The income dried up as his roles shifted, taking him from sought after roles of stature to menial tasks for pittance, to. . . nothing.

What was it that Jyrl was afflicted with? First, it was the obvious anxieties of irrational fears. Perhaps hallucinations, maybe they weren't, but he hoped on all things holy they were. That he could deal with. Or sometimes he could.

Sometimes, he would pull at his graying hair, holding back any tears that welled up, just trying to feel something other than fear. He'd just try to remind himself that those things that were around him flying, creeping, and crawling weren't really there.

Flying creatures, the kind that could bring a horrible death, were in the corners of his eyes. Bites that often go unnoticed, picked at his skin and nerves. Was it a bite or just a harmless mark that had always been there? He'd find a measure of comfort if he could test the area, the spot on his skin, and then another black flying creature would swoop into his peripheral vision undoing any progress that he had made.

These creatures, not there in reality, but to Jyrl, they were to be found in every dark recess, crevasse, and unseen nook. He would often ask those around him if they saw them, too. Jyrl could only do that so many times before people would question it. That's how Jyrl decided to just assume that it was all figments of his imagination. An imagination that had always been vivid and strong.

But now, instead of inventing stories and spells, he was inventing visions that felt much more real. Horrible things. Visions that made those hallucinations seem tame. He would rather have the hallucinations than to question if those other thoughts, vividly horrible, were real.

He couldn't pinpoint when or how it all began, though he tried like hell to do so. Sometimes, he thought that things were turning around and getting better, and then a dark episode would bring a shadow over his mind and then he was back to a crumbling man, engulfed in an internal turmoil that pushed him to the brink of tears and pain. Eight years of this mental anguish took its toll.

However, that isn't the story. At least not the whole of it.

Jyrl lived peacefully in a sparsely populated temple. He liked that. There were other mages there. That helped him keep a sort of sanity, knowing that others were around. But, and very importantly, he wasn't bothered. He wasn't sought after. He had chores to do, and that's when he would be summoned, but that was very rarely. Often, Jyrl wouldn't be spoken to for long stretches of time and never by name.

In recent months, it seemed that most everyone else left Jyrl alone. As long as he did the chores, Jyrl assumed, then he was pulling his weight. However, that was something he took a newfound joy in. A focus that would pull his weary mind away from its constant battle. He also found that in books.

His time was spent mostly on those two tasks. Chores and reading. His physical space was his room. Small, bright, and cool. It helped him, because, though the intentions of everyone that offered the advice to go out and walk in nature were good, that drove Jyrl to return to that dark place. Nature wasn't helpful. Walking about within it was a terrible idea. The books, a small quiet room, and daily routine were not terrible. He also had the benefits of many medicinal herbs from the temple grounds, that helped him to ease any anxieties.

His favorite chore involved sweeping the library floors. Often he could find a few good books or scrolls to read. Most of the people he saw might offer a smile, usually however, they just left him alone. His walks to the library were brisk, under the tall tower of the grand mage. A magnificent centerpiece of the temple. Five hundred feet tall, and sixty-five feet in diameter. It was crowned with a beautiful marble walkway at the top, overlooking the deep valley.

In all, the temple had been a place for healing and routine for Jyrl. If time was willing, he'd be able to regain his old self and rejoin the rest of the world one day.

Jyrl was lying on his bed when a knock came one night, just after sunset. Jyrl looked out the window and saw a man standing in the hall of the temple. He didn't recognize the person, but for him to be in the temple; he had to have been allowed in.

"Yes," Jyrl said after opening the door and seeing the unfamiliar man.

The man was robed, hooded in a black cowl, and tall. He brushed past Jyrl and took a seat across from Jyrl's bed. Jyrl eyed the man suspiciously. No matter what had happened in his life, Jyrl never lost his hot-blooded personality. That was what had helped propel him so young, but perhaps that was part of the problem that he felt now.

"Who are you?"

"Good evening, Jyrl. You don't know me, though that's not surprising. Most don't really know me," the hooded man said. The hooded man lifted his cowl and looked rather unremarkable, and Jyrl certainly didn't recognize him.

"See? Not surprising that you are finding it hard to place my face."

Jyrl shook his head. "I really can't. No matter, how can I help you?"

"You can't. You can't help anyone. You are cracked, your mind is turning into a mush that is reminiscent of porridge made of potatoes and rice. It is I that has come to help you. You called out to me and I'm here."

Jyrl furrowed his brow. "You have me confused with someone else. I didn't call on you."

"You did. Your prayers to be healed."

"I..." Jyrl thought a moment. "I only ever prayed, years ago, to Ema and the Creator. You are certainly not the Goddess of Wisdom, Ema. She is... well... you don't carry the visage of a woman."

"And of the other?"

"Are you the Creator?"

"What if I'm not?"

"Then what would you be?"

"Maybe the question is whom am I?"

Jyrl looked confused again. "Then who are you?"

"I am the third option."

Jyrl chuckled. "I didn't know I had options."

The man stood, matching Jyrl's height now. "There are always options, Jyrl. You had three. You called to the Creator. You then called to Ema, our mother of wisdom. Finally, and thirdly, you silently called to me."

"There were more than a few times that I prayed for..." Jyrl thought. "No. You couldn't be."

"I am."

"I haven't spoken those words for some time."

"Recently enough for me to be here, though. I've come to offer you the death, the respite, that you've begged for."

Jyrl shook his head rather frantically. "No! Not now! I'm feeling better."

"Are you?"

"I am. I can show you." Jyrl begged.

"What would you showing me your little world do to sway me? I've seen grandeur that you could only dream of, and I've seen humbleness that would bring you to tears. Your little world," he motioned around the room. "Though quaint and nice for you, is rather unremarkable to my goals here tonight."

"I think that if we speak, you will see things differently."

The hooded man shook his head. "The night is growing late, and you are not the only one I plan to visit."

"A chance to show that I don't want to go. That's all I ask."

The man looked at Jyrl. "I can spare a moment," he looked about the room and spotted a game board. It was a King's Table game. "Maybe just one game," he said, pointing at the game.

Jyrl nodded rapidly. "Yes, yes! That will do. I win and we part ways here and now, with nothing of note."

The man nodded under his hood. "And if I win, we leave this place together in respect."

Jyrl grinned. "Agreed," he said, setting the game up on a stool between the chair and the bed. "Please

13

note that I am rather skilled and familiar with the game."

"As am I, though it has been a century or two since I've played it."

The pair sat across from each other and began. Jyrl held the red pieces, while the stranger held the blue. Jyrl moved first. Though it was common for the guest to move first, the man had relinquished that custom to Jyrl. The game was not so quick.

Jyrl looked at the man as he was about to move a piece to the adjacent slot.

"It isn't easy dealing with all of this," Jyrl said, motioning to his head.

"Others do."

"Just because others might, doesn't mean I can as easily."

"I never said it was easy."

Jyrl's eyes narrowed. In part because of the conversation and because of his mental plan for the next move. He picked up a red piece and then took a blue piece as a prize for a successful maneuver.

"I wish I could figure out how it all happened," Jyrl said.

"Most do when they realize things have progressed further than they can manage," the stranger said, taking one of Jyrl's pieces. "It would not matter. The fact is, the damage is done. You've dealt with some form of mental anguish since child-hood. Perhaps, once long ago, you could have repaired it, but now..."

"It's too late?" Jyrl asked, pulling a piece back from danger.

The man nodded. He pursued Jyrl's nine remaining pieces.

Jyrl made another move and took yet another blue piece. He smiled at his cleverness. Something of the old Jyrl reared up within him. The man responded with another move, defensive to protect his more important pieces. Jyrl struck out and took another blue piece from the board.

The stranger, now with fewer pieces, moved his own pieces to the flanks, catching on to Jyrl's ploy. They each took their turns, removing pieces, and moving around the board in a cat-and-mouse style of play. Jyrl smiled with each move, toying with his visitor until he felt he had played his victorious hand.

"It seems that you might be walking away empty-handed," Jyrl smirked.

"Will I?" the man replied.

Jyrl started to chuckle but then looked down at the board. His king was trapped and any sort of help that the other pieces could provide was too far out to reach him in time.

He was surprised and unsure how he had made such an error. "I don't understand," Jyrl softly whispered.

The stranger stood as he removed Jyrl's king from the board. "I've come with respect and won't dishonor that by lying to you. This is your destiny. I don't come to take you away for any purpose of malice or anything other than what must be done."

"I don't want this."

"Most do not, but it is your time."

"What of my family? My children."

"Jyrl…" the man began. "How long do you think you have been in this temple?"

"Three years."

"Three years?"

Jyrl nodded. "I came here three years ago, after spending five years tormenting those around me. I ran away, hoping to return to them one day."

The man shook his head. "It has been more than three years since you arrived, Jyrl."

"No, I've been keeping track of my time," Jyrl stood. "See here?" he turned to a calendar, but he couldn't find it. "It was here along this wall."

"It was. Once."

Jyrl looked at the man. "How many years has it been?" the realization of what was happening was dawning on him.

"If I say, know that I only mean to help ease you along."

"How many years?" Jyrl asked again.

"Three thousand."

Jyrl gasped. His breath was gone, and he began to hyperventilate. He crouched low and tried to suck in as much air as he could breathe. Jyrl stood back up and bolted from his room. The shock of the outer temple complex tore his heart in two.

"What?!" he shouted, seeing the world around him.

A ruined temple stood before him. Crumbling rocks, stones long ago covered in moss, greeted him as he hurriedly stepped out of his room. The once great tower in the center of the temple, standing above the enormous library, was half destroyed by time and half destroyed by a creeping mass of nature taking the rocks and land back.

The library was nothing but a tomb for centuries of knowledge that could now be lost. He looked around and saw nothing was there. No one was around, and the entire complex was a mess of ruin and deterioration.

"This is what you have asked me to take you away from. Besides, it is a long time," the stranger said, walking up behind Jyrl.

"Why now, after so long?"

The stranger sighed. "Mages, like yourself, have ways to prolong the inevitable. I don't meddle in such affairs; however, you lost control of it and prolonged your days much more than any other mage."

"The temple is gone. I was just sweeping the library halls this morning."

"No," the stranger said. "You haven't swept those halls in centuries."

The stranger stepped in front of Jyrl. "Think of this complex, shattered and ruined, as your mind. Still here, physically here, but unrepairable unless with great effort. You went too far trying to forget any torment from within yourself by dosing on poppy and night-honey. You delved too deeply into a world not of your own making, but within yourself. That was why you slept so long. Still, to this day, this very moment, you sleep."

"I'm not asleep," Jyrl scoffed. "I'm wide awake here in the middle of what once was my home."

"You are asleep still, breathing your last, but this was never your home."

"I'm still asleep?" Jyrl felt the heavy but somewhat comforting weight of tiredness come over him.

The stranger nodded. "For but a moment more."

"What happens next?"

"That is up to you. This is but one journey in the universe of countless journeys that one might take. When you awake again, your next journey will begin," the stranger said.

Jyrl smiled softly. He looked back to his room and nodded before turning back toward the stranger and walking off, and away from what had once been his small room. A place of routine and comfort away from the world.

And left there, resting on the bed, was Jyrl's final game piece, the king.

* * *

Joseph S. Samaniego is a father, hubby, author, publisher, gamer, historian, and all around the world ne'er do well in some eyes. To most, he's just another raconteur spinning tales. Enjoy, and be well!

Image

Coming

Soon

Court Date

By Kent J. Moore

I usually welcome a beautiful woman joining me at dinner. Jessie was an exception.

I sat alone at the usual table and listened to a violinist and cellist play Bach in a corner of my favorite Kansas City restaurant. Suddenly, a pair of bare arms embraced me from behind, causing me to splash some of my after-dinner port on the linen tablecloth.

A smoldering voice sighed in my ear, "Nicholas, I am so glad I found you. I need your help."

I recoiled from the unwanted hug as Jessie slid into the chair next to mine. Her auburn hair hung down to the deep neckline of her black dress. I diverted my eyes only to catch her wavy hemline as it slid up the thighs of her long legs.

I adjusted my tie and the cuffs of my navy blazer before responding.

"It's been four years. When we broke up, you said you didn't need me anymore. In fact, you said if you ever saw me again, it'd be too soon." I sipped more of my port. "Besides, it's Friday night. I'm on a date."

"My husband is missing. I want to retain your services to find him."

"Why me?"

"As I recall, you are the best at what you do."

I started to open my mouth, and she put two fingers across my lips.

"And before you make some lewd double entendre, I meant as a private investigator. I have no one else to whom I can turn."

"What about the police?" I asked.

"I called them. They said he had not been gone long enough to be a 'missing person.' I cannot wait that long. Who knows what might befall him between now and then?"

I shook my head. "I don't know. How'd you find me?"

She gave me a carnivorous smile and dismissive wave of her hand. "I have my sources."

"That doesn't—"

Another woman appeared at the table. "I step away to the ladies' room for five minutes, and you replace me?" Like a silver bell being rung, the voice and its owner demanded attention.

Jessie eyed the newcomer, whose sleeveless red dress showed off well-toned arms and legs but was otherwise less daring than Jessie's number. "Is this your date, Nicholas? My God, she's young enough to be—"

"His wife," the other woman said. "And you?"

When it rains, it pours. In my case, it felt more like a monsoon. I stood, at which point a saner man might have retreated. Instead, I charged ahead.

"This is Courtney Kilpatrick, also known as Mrs. Nick Alexander." I turned to my wife. "Court, this is an old acquaintance of mine, Jessica Beech." I looked at Jessie, remembering she'd gotten married since I'd seen her last. "Is it still 'Beech'?"

She nodded.

To be fair, Court was 15 years younger than me. Her petite stature and blonde, pixie hairstyle made her look even younger. I occasionally wondered what she saw in me, a fifty-year old whose dark brown crewcut was flecked with gray and whose six-foot frame was beginning to sag around the middle.

To the accompaniment of clattering dishes and people talking around them, the two women eyed each other over the demilitarized zone of our table. Jessie extended a hand.

"Pleased to meet you. Nicholas is being modest. We are more than acquaintances. We are, in fact, former lovers, and for the record, I'm just as 'old' as he is, which is not old at all in my book. And please, do call me 'Jessie.' All my friends do."

Court resumed her seat across from mine. "Yeah, well ... Jessica, what brings you to our table this evening?"

"My husband, Martin, has gone missing. I want Nicholas to find him."

"When'd you last see him?" Court asked.

"Don't answer that," I said to Jessie as I scowled at Court. "I'm not investigating his disappearance."

Jessie ignored me. "I last saw him yesterday morning, as he left for work. When he didn't come home last night, I became worried. This morning, I called his office. They haven't seen him since Wednesday. They said he called in sick yesterday."

"Where's he work?" Court asked.

"The Atlantic Edible Seaweed Company."

"You're kidding, right? Seriously, where's he work?" Court asked.

Jessie reached into her purse and produced a business card, which she set between Court and me. The words "Atlantic Edible Seaweed Company" and their logo stretched across the top, below which was "Martin Atwater," along with his title and contact information. I looked at Court, who just shrugged back at me.

Our waiter appeared with the chocolate cake I'd ordered earlier. Court had insisted she didn't want dessert. Now, the waiter asked Jessie, "May I offer you anything, ma'am?"

I waved a hand at the waiter. "The lady isn't staying."

"Nick!" Court frowned.

"That's quite all right. I'm feeling too distraught to eat or drink anything," Jessie said. The waiter took his cue and left.

Court looked at me. "Aren't you going to ask anything?"

I shrugged. "Why? Already said it's not my case. Besides, you're doing okay without me."

Court resumed questioning Jessie. "Would anybody want to hurt him?"

"Martin borrowed money from a loan shark."

My curiosity got the best of me as I picked up a forkful of cake. "This shark have a name?"

"Yes, he does, but unfortunately, I don't know it. Martin simply called him 'Jaws'."

Court laughed. When neither Jessie nor I did, she said, "What? It's funny. A loan 'shark' named Jaws." She reached across the table and took a bite of my cake.

"I thought you didn't want dessert," I said to Court.

"I didn't want a whole dessert. Just a bite."

I returned my attention to Jessie. "How much did he borrow, and why?"

"I don't know."

"Anything else?" Court asked.

Jessie began to sniffle and grabbed my napkin to dab her eyes, although I didn't see any tears. "No. I just really want my Martin home safely. I'm completely adrift without him, and I'll do almost anything to get him back." She laid a well-manicured hand on one of mine and looked at me. "Almost anything."

"Don't worry. Nick'll find him." Court resumed eating my cake.

"Of that, I have no doubt," Jessie said.

I extracted my hand from Jessie's and folded my arms across my chest. "If I do look for him, and I'm not saying I will, I still charge a thousand dollars a day plus expenses. First day's paid in advance. Plus, an extra day's pay if I find him." I threw the last bit in on a whim, just to see how desperate she was.

She produced ten hundred-dollar bills from her purse and tucked them in my shirt pocket, her hand lingering on my chest and her face inches from mine. "Please consider yourself hired. If you need or want anything to find my Martin . . . Just let me know."

Jessie pulled her cell phone from her purse and tapped the screen a few times.

"I just texted you a picture of Martin. Thank you, Nicholas. I can't wait to hear from you." Before leaving, she gave me a kiss on the cheek, her perfume and proximity overpowering. I still had questions but let them go as my heart pounded beneath the crisp bills stretching my shirt.

I stole a glance across the table at Court. She just rolled her eyes then turned to watch as Jessie strutted to the door.

"Jessica has left the building," Court deadpanned.

I dipped my napkin in what remained of my ice water and tried to scrub off Jessie's scarlet lipstick. "What's the big idea, telling her I'd find him?"

"I know you too well, Nick. You're going to help her in the end. You totally can't stop it. You've got a thing for damsels in distress. That's how we met. Remember?"

"She's not in distress. Her attempt at tears was as phony as your last commercial. Hell, I'd be surprised if she's even married. This is probably all some wild goose chase." I reached for the cake with my fork and discovered there was nothing left but some stray crumbs and ganache.

Court licked incriminating chocolate from her lips. "Like, who pays a thousand bucks to send you on a wild goose chase? If she wanted to do that, she'd have just told you one of the Kardashian's is in town with Britney Spears."

"I still kick myself for falling for that one. Since when do you want me to help an old girlfriend? Didn't you see her coming on to me?"

"Well, someone has an inflated opinion of himself. Aren't you being just a bit too cynical? Besides, it's not like I'm going to let you go alone." She used my fork to collect the remnants of cake and ganache from my plate.

"What's that supposed to mean?"

"Means I'll go with you."

"Now, hold on—"

"I've always wanted to see how a real private eye works. You are a real one, aren't you?"

"That's what my license says." I pushed away the empty dessert plate.

"Also, my agent got me an audition for a detective role in a TV pilot. This would be a terrific experience heading into the audition. We'd be totally great as a team. Kind of like Jennifer Aniston and Adam Sandler in that Netflix movie we saw last week."

"You're comparing me to Adam Sandler?"

"No, I'm comparing me to a younger Jennifer Aniston, like when she was on *Friends*."

"Now who's got an inflated opinion of themselves?" I asked.

She stuck her tongue out at me.

"Doesn't matter. It's too dangerous."

"Bullshit!" She pointed an accusatory finger at me. "You always say you spend most of your time on the Internet, talking with people, or sitting in a car waiting and watching. You afraid I'll be bored to death?" She crossed her arms and dared me to disagree.

As a PI, I knew dull routine could turn ugly in a hurry. I also knew Court was correct about how I spent most of my time. She wouldn't let the matter go easily or be happy if I kept refusing. Our marriage was fresh enough I still aimed to please. Besides, my continued refusal might plant unwarranted seeds of doubt about Jessie and me. I'd save myself a lot of grief if I just surrendered now.

I raised my hands in mock defeat. "Oh, alright already, I'll look into Martin's alleged disappearance and let you tag along. Since you got me into this gig, you can help me get out of it. With any luck, we'll discover this is all some outrageous prank on her part. That said, if I think things are going south in a bad way at any point, you do exactly as I say when I say it, no questions asked. Understood?"

"Understood. We'll totally make a date of it. The

night's still young. So, where do we start?" She stood and stepped away from our table.

"Whoa there. Aren't you forgetting something?" I gestured to her purse, still hanging on the back of her chair. I signaled the waiter for the check then stood and gave Court a kiss. "We start by paying the bill. After that, we'll go see a shark about a loan."

* * *

From the restaurant, Court and I cruised over to The Grotto, a "gentleman's club" with an underwater theme Larry Flynt and Walt Disney might have concocted, if they'd ever worked together. A pudgy redhead, with a pair of strategically placed clamshells on top and a sequined skirt that hid little, gyrated to the Beach Boys' Kokomo on the central platform. I'd never view The Little Mermaid the same way.

I tried to hustle Court past the entertainment. Instead, she stopped to take in her surroundings.

"You certainly know how to show a girl a good time. Dinner and a show," she said.

"You wanted to ride along. Still want to see what a real PI does?"

"Sure. I noticed you didn't need to consult Siri for directions."

"You don't have anything to be jealous about."

Court cocked her head as she eyed the redhead on stage. "You're totally right about that."

From there, we moved to the back of The Grotto, past the restrooms, and up a flight of stairs. At the top, a droopy-eyed guy with a walrus mustache and figure to match guarded a door marked "Manager."

"Can I's help you?" he asked with a voice like a rock tumbler.

"We're here to see the manager," I said.

"He ain't available."

"Tell him Nick Alexander's here about a loan."

"Wait here." He slipped through the door and returned a minute later. "Okay, he'll see you. Lemme take your jacket." An order, not a request. I gave him my blazer. He patted me down, then reached for Court.

She slapped his hands before he could touch her. "Don't even think about it. If you want to cop a feel, you've got to put a ring on it." She held up her left hand in front of his face and pointed to me with her right. "And he already beat you to it."

Wincing behind the smile pasted to my face, I slipped between Court and the heavy. "You'll have to excuse her. She's a little high strung."

Court stepped out from behind me. "Who are you calling 'high strung'? Besides, what does he think I'm concealing in this outfit?" The sleeveless red dress left some things to the imagination, but hiding a gun wasn't one of them.

Our now wide-eyed greeter studied Court for a moment and came to the same conclusion. "Okay, but you's gotta at least let me see inside your purse."

Court opened her purse for his benefit, and he let us inside.

A haze hung in the air with the smell of stale

tobacco, and a bald man sat behind a glass-topped desk. His crisp, white suit didn't disguise the well-developed muscles underneath. Our host removed the cigar protruding from a corner of his mouth and flashed a smile full of teeth. Jaws.

I broke out in a sweat, despite the frigid temperature from the air conditioner's relentless effort against the summer heat outside. My stomach roiled at that smile and memories of other encounters with Jaws. I glanced over my shoulder as I tugged at my tie and ran a finger around the inside of my collar. Thankfully, the heavy had left. I looked at Court. She seemed unperturbed and surveyed the office with the same disdain she'd shown my apartment when we first met.

"Nicky, what a pleasant surprise," Jaws said, his deep bass resonating. He turned toward Court. "And who's this enchanting vision, new talent for The Grotto I hope?"

"As if," Court said. "Not that you couldn't use some from what I've seen." She stepped up to the desk and extended a hand. "I'm Courtney Kilpatrick, Nick's. . . Partner."

Jaws stood, dwarfing Court. "I'm pleased to meet you."

He enveloped the proffered hand in one of his. Now, it was Court's turn to wince. When he let go, she massaged one hand with the other.

"I haven't seen you for a while, Nicky. Please, have a seat." He motioned to two red leather chairs facing the desk as he retook his own. "How's the private investigations business?"

I shifted one of the chairs, so I could see both Jaws and the office door while seated. "It's going all right."

"I'm glad to hear that. But I thought my assistant outside said something about a loan? Are you in need of some financial assistance?"

"No, thanks. I'm good. I'm here about another client of yours. Guy named Martin Atwater. His wife thought you might've loaned him some money."

Jaws leaned back and played with his cigar. He studied us across the desk, his gray eyes betraying nothing. They appeared dull and lifeless. I knew better.

"The name sounds familiar. Of course, even if he was a client – and I'm not saying he is – I couldn't share any information with you. I need to respect my clients' confidentiality. I'm sure you remember that."

Court addressed me from the other chair. "You borrowed money from this person? So much for the wisdom of our elders." She turned to Jaws. "No offense."

"None taken," he said.

"Not all of us had a trust fund waiting for us when we were born," I said. "It was before I met you."

I knew the consequences for failing to pay Jaws, thankfully not from personal experience. Knowing the premium he placed on getting his money back — plus interest — I decided to try another tack.

"I understand you need to protect your clients. But Mr. Atwater's missing. . ."

Jaws leaned forward and rested his elbows on the desk, narrowing the gulf between him and us. His dull, lifeless eyes now had a hint of interest. "Missing?"

Court nodded. "Yeah, that's right. My partner and I are investigating his disappearance. We have no clue where he is at the moment."

"And no guarantee he'll repay any loan he has," I said.

Jaws leaned even farther over his desk as I continued.

"Maybe his lender figured Mr. Atwater wasn't good for it and made him disappear."

Jaws' shoulders went slack, like a line after the fish has slipped the hook. He leaned back, again, flashing us a toothy grin.

"Now, Nicky, you know that isn't how it's done. A borrower that sleeps with the fishes, so to speak, is not good for business. The loan goes unpaid, and it discourages other potential customers." He took a long drag on his cigar and blew a stream of smoke into the office haze. "Of course, a borrower who doesn't pay his debt isn't good for business, either. If he's missing, I suspect his lender would be very interested to find him. Very interested."

"How interested?" I asked

"I feel the lender would be interested enough to provide a lead. . . For a price."

"What's the going rate for a lead in a missing person's case?" Court asked.

"$400," Jaws said

I started to reach for my wallet. Court laid a hand on my arm and said, "That's unfortunate. We only pay a hundred."

I gritted my teeth and tried not to clench my hands as I looked first at her then Jaws. The latter broke into another full-fledged smile as he stood and started pacing around the room, the plush red carpet absorbing the impact and sound of his steps. Only the distant beat of the pulsing music downstairs disturbed the silence.

Jaws stopped next to Court's chair. "I suspect you haven't purchased a lead before, have you?"

"Yeah, I have, and Nick's purchased more than me. We might be prepared to pay more than $100, but we're not about to pay $400."

I knew Jaws enjoyed the hunt as much as the kill, and I wanted to leave him happy. Hell, I just wanted to leave alive.

"This is all hypothetical," I said with a dismissive wave of my hand. "Maybe you're not the guy to supply a lead. Maybe the guy who is would sell us one for less than $400."

Jaws was almost giddy as he resumed circling. "If I sold you a lead on Mr. Atwater, it would be worth $400."

"What kind of lead's worth that much?" Court asked

"It's the kind that tells you why he needed the loan and who may know more about that."

That did sound valuable, but Court still wasn't ready to give Jaws the satisfaction he craved. "Well, maybe that's worth more than $100, but four still seems high. How about two? One for why and one for who."

Jaws chuckled, and the predatory smile gave way to one that seemed to reflect genuine amusement. I hadn't seen this side of Jaws before. I wasn't sure whether to be relieved or even more afraid.

"Ms. Kilpatrick, this isn't Walmart. I only deal in the best, and the best is worth more than $200. However, given my past relationship with Nicky and since I like your moxie, I'm going to offer you a one-time discount and settle for $300."

"Sold," I said, sensing it was his final offer and having nothing else to go on. If it led us to Martin, Jessie's bonus would more than cover the asking price. I might even be able to expense it with her. I pulled three one-hundred-dollar bills from my wallet and laid them on the desktop. Jaws quit circling.

"Now, for the record, I'm not saying Mr. Atwater is or was my client. However, in my business, I hear things, and I just remembered where I heard Mr. Atwater's name before. Rumor has it he liked to bet with Ambassador Marwick. Do you know The Ambassador, Nicky? Of course, you do. Everyone knows him. Anyway, it could be Mr. Atwater lost a lot of money, some of which wasn't his own, and he needed a loan to cover up his. . . misappropriation until his luck turned. That's all I know."

Jaws continued, "Like I say, borrowers who don't pay their debts are not good for business." The voice was stern now, less gregarious. "If someone loaned Mr. Atwater some funds he wasn't inclined to repay by going missing, I'm sure the lender would be very appreciative of whoever found him. His return could be worth well more than $300, if you catch my drift." Jaws opened the door and motioned to his assistant, who returned my jacket as we left.

As we stepped outside The Grotto, I grabbed Court's elbow. "Why were you haggling in there? I had the money to pay what Jaws was asking. You trying to get us killed?"

"Nobody pays retail anymore. I just saved us a hundred dollars for our next fine dining experience. I think what you mean to say is 'Thank you, Dear.' And by the way. . .You're welcome."

I rolled my eyes. "Thank you, Dear. In the future, please give me a heads up when you're about to do something I may regret."

"How?"

"Call me some ridiculous nickname like 'Chuckles' or 'Ace'."

"Okay, but isn't a nickname for a guy named 'Nick' redundant? Where to from here?"

"We'll join The Ambassador for a nightcap. Maybe he can tell us something. For Martin's sake, we better find him before Jaws does."

* * *

Court frowned at the establishment in front of us. "You said we were going for a nightcap."

"I did. I didn't say it would be alcoholic."

"Yeah, but. . . IHOP? What's an ambassador doing here?"

"Well, it is an 'international' house of pancakes."

I ushered Court inside. Unlike The Grotto, IHOP was relatively quiet, the soft murmur of conversation broken occasionally by clattering dishes and a beeping cash register near the front doors. I scanned the sparse crowd until I found who I was looking for, then led Court toward his booth in the back.

Hunkered down in the booth was a scrawny man in his early sixties with a greasy, gray comb-over the hue of yellow sputum. Thick, black-framed glasses rested near the tip of his nose. Sid "The Ambassador" Marwick stared at a laptop on the table while talking on a cell phone. When the call was done, he forked the last of a Belgian waffle into his mouth, his attention still on the laptop and one hand tapping away at the keys. We slid onto the opposite bench.

"Beat it. Booth's taken," he said, not looking at us. The high-pitched voice was as thin and reedy as the man to whom it belonged.

"He's not very diplomatic," Court whispered.

"Hence, the irony of his title," I whispered back. "Sid, it's me. Nick."

He looked up, his middle finger pushing his glasses to the bridge of his nose. I wondered whether he was subconsciously or intentionally flipping me off. "Mr. Nick, long time, no see. Who's your friend?"

"This is Mrs. Nick."

Court extended a hand and a smile to Sid. "Hi, I'm Ms. Kilpatrick, Nick's better half, but please call me 'Courtney'. I think 'Mrs. Nick' is his mother."

"Nice to meetcha. What's a nice girl like you doin' with this guy?" He jerked a thumb in my direction.

"I ask myself that all the time," Court said with a wink.

"Wanna bet on the Royals?" Sid asked me.

"No, I'll wait for the Chiefs to start."

"Smart move. Better return on investment. . . When they win."

Only Sid used "return on investment" to describe winning a bet. The bookie was an accountant at heart, which is why I also let him do my taxes.

A waitress joined us. "Like to see a menu?" she asked Court and me.

"No, just bring me some decaf." I turned to Court. "And you, Dear?"

"I'd like some orange juice, please."

Sid pushed his empty plate toward the waitress. "How 'bout Swedish crepes for dessert?"

When the waitress was gone, I said, "I'm looking for Martin Atwater."

Sid's attention returned to the laptop screen. "Don't know him."

"Not the way I heard it."

"You heard wrong."

I leaned back and spread my arms along the top edge of the back of the bench. "I'll tell Jaws you said so."

Sid shuddered. "Not good if I go 'round fingerin' guys."

"Understood. Except, this guy's missing and owes Jaws money. Jaws pointed us at you. If you don't point us somewhere that leads to this guy, maybe I tell Jaws you wouldn't help find someone who owes him." I glanced at my wristwatch then back at Sid. "So, what's it going to be?"

He frowned. "Jeez Louise, what'd I do to deserve that? Bad enough the state's legalizin' sports bets and people just gamble online. I'm gonna go bust soon as it is."

Court turned to me. "Yeah, Nick. Why are you being so hard on Sid?" She reached across the table and patted one of his hands.

"Because, I want to close this case, and Jaws says Sid may know something."

The waitress returned with our drinks. I took a sip of my coffee. Court slipped a travel-size bottle of vodka from her purse and added it to the OJ. I leaned over to her. "Who says you're not handy? You know how to handle a screwdriver."

She stuck her tongue out at me. "Screw you."

"I certainly hope so," I said.

"You two wanna get a room?" Sid asked, closing his laptop. "Now, gimme that name, again?"

"Martin Atwater." I showed him the picture Jessie had texted me.

"Oh yeah, him. Hit it big on the Cubbies Wednesday. Collected his winnings and split with that cute little number of his."

"His wife?" I asked.

"Doubt it. Barely legal, I bet. Kinda like...." He flicked his eyes in Court's direction.

She smiled at Sid. "I'm flattered you think I'm that young. Does this girl have a name?"

"'Fiona,' he called her. No last name. Just 'Fiona'."

"That's all you've got?" I asked.

"Swear on my mother's grave, if she was dead."

Sid was many things. A good liar wasn't one of them. What little he'd given us was the truth.

"So, what're you gonna tell Jaws?" Sid asked.

"Don't worry. You're covered. I'll tell Jaws you were helpful whether we find Atwater or not."

Court patted his hand again. "Don't worry. I'll vouch for you. Jaws likes me. He thinks I have 'moxie,' whatever that is."

Sid wiped his forehead with a napkin as the waitress delivered his crepes. "Thanks." His cell phone rang, and he answered it. "Sid. Whatcha want?"

We left him to his international cuisine and headed for the car. Court stifled a yawn.

"I think we've had enough fun for one night," I said, opening her door for her.

"That works for me. I'm super tired."

"Let's get a good night's sleep. We'll scope out Martin's employer in the morning." I pointed to her purse. "When we do, pack an extra bottle for me. I may need something to wash down my edible seaweed."

* * *

Next morning, Kim Kardashian, Britney Spears, and I were about to do something I'm sure is illegal when Court shook my shoulder and said, "Wake up, Nick. We need to get going."

I rolled over in bed and forced one eye open. Court stood fully dressed in designer jeans, white blouse, and camel-colored blazer, a steaming mug in one hand.

I closed my eye, again. "You're not bleeding. The house better be burning. Otherwise, you're in serious trouble. What the hell time is it, anyway?"

"It's eight o'clock. Atlantic Edible Seaweed opens at nine. They're only open till noon on Saturdays, so you need to get a move on." She set the mug on the night table next to me. The aroma of fresh roast hazelnut opened both eyes this time. "I made a list of questions to ask when we get there. Hopefully, someone can give us a new lead on Martin or the mysterious Fiona."

I sandwiched two mugs of coffee and a sesame bagel around a long shower amid 30 minutes in the bathroom. Then, I donned khaki slacks, button-up shirt, and blazer of my own for our drive to a nondescript office building in the suburbs. Atlantic Edible Seaweed's offices were behind two glass doors opposite the elevators on the third floor.

A petite, teenage brunette in a white polo with the company logo on it stood behind a counter separating her from the rest of reception area. She exuded a warm smile and light, fruity scent as we approached.

"Good morning! Welcome to Atlantic Edible Seaweed. Like, how can I help you?" She delivered the chipper, rapid-fire greeting in a voice that approached the sound of a blender set on "High."

I smiled back. "Good morning, Ms. . .," I glanced at the name plate on the receptionist's counter, "Ms. Galloway, could you—"

"Oh, like I'm not Fiona. My name's Emily. I'm just filling in, 'cause Fiona called in sick. Can I help you, sir?"

"I think you just did," I said. "We're looking for Ms. Galloway. Have a phone number or address where we could reach her? It's important."

Emily's eyes narrowed, and her nose crinkled as a note of doubt crept into her voice. "I'm. . . I'm not sure. Like, who are you?"

I typically feel honesty is the best policy. However, sometimes, improvisation has its place.

Court must have felt the same. She pushed in front of me, chest out and shoulders back, addressing Emily in a drawl that would have made any Southern belle proud. "I'm Dr. O'Hara with the Centers for Disease Control in Atlanta." As I rolled my eyes behind her, Court pulled out the Actors Equity membership card she kept in an embossed leather holder and flashed it just long enough for Emily to see something official without, apparently, registering what it was.

Court motioned toward me. "This here is my associate, Mr. Butler." I offered a wan smile, wondering where Court was going with this charade.

"Is Mr. Atwater. . . Martin Atwater around?" Court asked.

Emily shook her head. "No, but—."

Court frowned. "Oh, he's unavailable, too. That's unfortunate and a most ominous sign." She extracted her cell phone from a blazer pocket and began randomly tapping icons without letting Emily see the screen.

"What kind of sign? Like, is something wrong with Fiona and Mr. Atwater?"

Court held the cell phone up so Emily still couldn't see the screen then moved it slowly up and down in front of the receptionist, frowning and shaking her head in the process. Emily put her hands on the countertop and stretched without success to view what was on Court's phone.

"What's wrong?" Emily asked.

From my perspective, everything in this scenario was wrong. However, Emily seemed to be buying Court's story. I bit my lip and let it ride.

"Just how long have you been at Ms. Galloway's station?" Court asked.

"Since Thursday." Beads of perspiration had broken out on her forehead.

"I see," Court said. "And in that time, have you experienced any headaches, nausea, perspiration, respiration, or sleep disturbances?"

"Well, I did have a totally creepy nightmare last night. Oh, and my tummy felt weird yesterday. Course, I had kung pao chicken for lunch. I almost never get that." She ran a hand across her forehead. "Now, I'm sweating." She held out her palm, so we could see the moisture.

"Oh my God in Heaven," Court stepped back from the counter, pulling me with her, "I do declare, you have it, too."

"What? What do I have?"

"You show unmistakable signs of Red Tide Syndrome, just like we heard from Mr. Atwater and Ms. Galloway. You probably picked it up from workin' at her station."

Now, Emily stepped back from the counter. Her wide eyes scanned the space as color drained from her face. "I do? Shit. What should I do?"

Court pointed at the glass entry doors. "You need to scoot on down to the restroom right away and wash any exposed skin as thoroughly as possible. Don't touch anythin' on the way. I'll be right there to give you my undivided attention just as soon as I direct my associate on what to do. We may need to call a containment unit and quarantine this here establishment. There's no time to waste. Hurry!"

Emily dashed across the reception area and hip-checked one of the glass doors open before scurrying in the direction of the restrooms, her arms held up like a doctor who'd just scrubbed for surgery.

As soon as Emily was out of sight, Court turned to me, her accent gone. "I'll keep her busy as long as I can. See if you can find an address or something for Fiona. When you do, text me, then I'll ditch our dupe and meet you back at the car." With that, she hustled after Emily.

I ducked behind the counter and rifled through papers on and in the desk until I found an insurance form with Fiona's name and address on it. "Jackpot," I whispered. I texted Court.

As promised, she met me at the car. "How's your patient?" I asked.

Court smiled. "She'll live."

"How come you're a doctor and I'm not?"

"Because it was my show, I'm the star, and it worked. Once again, I think what you mean to say is 'Thank you, dear'."

I gave her a quick kiss. "Thank you, dear. I'd still like a heads up when you're about to pull a stunt like that though."

"Oh yeah, the whole nickname thing. So, where we headed?"

I showed her the address on the insurance form.

"Great," Court said. "So. . . Chuckles, I've got an idea I'd like to run by you on the way."

Following Court's idea, we borrowed a pair of costumes from one of her theater friends and bought a box the size of a 100-gallon aquarium. We filled the box with packing peanuts and some bricks to give it heft then drove to Ms. Galloway's apartment. I knocked on the door as we stood there with the box between us.

A few moments later, a woman's voice with an Irish lilt and the timbre of someone who'd just inhaled helium, addressed us from behind the door. "Yeah, and who is it?"

"UPS," I said. "Package for Ms. Fiona Galloway."

"Ay, that's me. Just leave it. I'll get it later, yeah."

"No can do," I said. "Apparently, it's valuable, because it needs a signature. Otherwise, we have to take it with us."

The door opened as far as the chain latch inside would allow. A freckled face topped with hair dyed pink and purple peered at us. "'Valuable,' you say?"

"Yes, and heavy, too." We lifted the box and feigned it was all we could do to handle it.

The door closed long enough to unhook the chain then swung open wide. Fiona waved us inside and motioned to the living room floor. "Yeah, just set it there."

We deposited the box where Fiona indicated as she closed the door behind us. The living room flowed into a cozy dining area with a Windsor table and four matching chairs, to the left of which I could see a doorway to the kitchen.

Although late morning, Fiona was in a satin robe that barely reached to her thighs. She fumbled with the robe's sash, failing to cinch it very tight and giving us a peek at the lingerie underneath. She put her hands on her hips. "Well?" she asked.

"Well, what?" I asked.

"And where do I sign, yeah?"

Court flourished a phony invoice we'd created. "Right here. Do you have ID?"

"'ID', you say?" Fiona tilted her head and scratched her temple.

"Yeah," Court said. "Just because the invoice says 'Fiona Galloway' at this address doesn't make you Fiona Galloway." Court patted the top of the box. "Have to make sure it gets to the right person."

"Honestly! Of all the. . ." Fiona threw up her hands and muttered to herself as she headed down an adjacent hallway, presumably to find some identification. Court trailed after her and pointed me in the direction of the dining room and kitchen.

In the kitchen, a wall clock showed it was eleven-thirty. The remnants of breakfast still littered the island countertop. Ten toes peeked out from behind one end of the island.

"Come on out," I said. "I see you."

Our quarry stood, clad only in a pair of plaid boxers, his eyes wide and hands shaking. "Who're you? Who sent you?" He shook his head. "Doesn't matter. Give you a thousand bucks to forget me long enough to get away."

I started to ask for an explanation when something hit me on the back of the head. Everything went black.

* * *

When I regained consciousness, Jessie was standing in the doorway to the kitchen holding a Glock nine-millimeter in her well-manicured right hand. A brown leather handbag stuffed with cash sat on the floor next to her. The kitchen wall clock behind her showed 15 minutes had elapsed. I became aware I was seated in one of the Windsor chairs, and someone was tying my hands to the spindles that formed the chair's back. Martin and Court were lashed to two of the other chairs.

"Found him," I said to Jessie. "How'd you get in here?"

"An attentive woman learns things when she dates a private investigator, like how to pick a lock."

Fiona came from behind my chair, her arms raised in the universal "Don't shoot, I surrender" formation. Tears trickled down her cheeks, and she blubbered a little as Jessie motioned with the Glock for her to sit in the remaining chair. Jessie gave a quick tug on my bonds. Satisfied, she proceeded to tie up Fiona and resumed her place by the cash-filled handbag.

My head was still swimming as I tried to focus on Jessie. "What gives?"

"Martin gives, and I take. He spent almost every dollar we owned on horse races, dog races, football games. . . you name it. When he finally managed to pick a winner, he decided to share the proceeds with this. . . bimbo," she aimed the gun at Fiona, "rather than the woman who faithfully supported him "til death do us part'." She turned to Martin. "Well, death is about to part us, Dear."

"What's that got to do with Court and me?" I asked. "Way I see it, we didn't cheat you. Didn't cheat on you either. We just want our fee for finding Martin. What you do with him after that's your business. No need for collateral damage." I glanced over at Court, her lips pursed and eyes wide, fixed on Jessie and the Glock. I returned my attention to Jessie. "What do you, say?"

"I say that's a nice thought, but if I'm tying up loose ends, I may as well tie up all of them."

"Somehow, that doesn't surprise me. How'd you find us?" I asked.

"The same way I did at the restaurant last night. When we were a couple, we allowed each other to know where the other was via our phones. I thought it romantic that you cared that much. Now, I wonder whether you simply didn't trust me. Regardless, I discovered you never changed things on your phone, so I followed you through mine."

Whatever bound me to the chair kept me from slapping my forehead. I made a mental note to have Court help me update my phone if we somehow got out of this mess. I glanced back over at her. The lips remained pursed, but her eyes, still fixed on Jessie, had taken on a studious, concentrated look.

As Jessie turned her attention to Martin, Court said, "Don't worry. . . Chuckles. . . we'll get out of this. . . somehow." She moved her hands out from behind the back of her chair long enough for me to see they were untied then slipped them behind the chair, again. Fiona was no better at tying hands than she was the sash of her robe.

Sweat beaded on Martin's forehead like condensation on a beer mug. He cringed as Jessie kissed him hard on the lips, but he was in no position to do more than that.

Jessie said, "Good-bye, Dear. Remember, 'You always hurt the one you love'." She stepped back and raised the Glock.

Martin wasn't the only one sweating up a storm now. I decided to try a little improv of my own. "Before you off this guy, I want him to hear you answer something for me. Who'd you love more: him or me?"

Jessie rolled her eyes. "Nicholas, please don't tell me you are jealous of this loser."

"No, but I noticed you gave him quite a smooch while I'm just sucking air over here."

"Maybe she's expecting you to pay her for one," Court said, nodding at the bag of cash. "Look how much Martin's cost. I'll bet she's done way more for less with others though."

Jessie ignored the jibe and walked around the table, staring down at me, the pistol pointed at my chest. "Nicholas, you were special to me once, more than Martin here could have ever hoped to be. However, that was then, and this is now. Still, I have every intention of enjoying one last kiss before you die."

She lowered the Glock and leaned in for the kiss. As she did, I tilted my head back as if to receive it and then snapped it forward as hard as I could into the bridge of her nose. An audible crack was followed by a spray of blood from both nostrils and a string of expletives as she keeled backward, dropping the Glock in the process. Court leaped up, kicked the pistol in my direction, and used her chair to pin Jessie to the floor, sitting on it for good measure, until I was able to free myself with Fiona's help.

Later, after we called the cops and they took Jessie away for attempted murder, Martin thanked us for saving his life. Fiona gave me a long hug, which I returned with equal gusto while Court crossed her arms with an exasperated sigh.

As Court and I drove home, I said, "Sorry about all that. I should never—"

"Are you kidding? That was amazing! We knocked 'em dead, as we say in the business. I can't wait for our next case."

I rubbed my forehead. The headache induced by head butting Jessie seemed to be getting worse with Court's reaction. "I've created a monster."

"Yes, but I'm your monster." She leaned across the seat and kissed me on the cheek. "Plus, I don't charge for kisses. Now, if you want more than that. . ."

I laughed and wondered what my next Court date might entail.

* * *

Kent J. Moore is an author and consultant living in Kansas. His work appears in FPM, a peer-reviewed journal of the American Academy of Family Physicians; Humanities, the

National Endowment for the Humanities' magazine; Stories from the Lockdown, an anthology to benefit UNICEF's VaccinAid; and the horror anthology, From the Yonder 4. Two of his short stories have won local writing contests.

WHY DO YOU
ALWAYS

3/8   3/8

BEAT UP THE
LITTLE GUY

by J. D. Lorentson

Why Do You Always Beat Up the Little Guys?

By J. D. Lorentson

Jim cursed as his four broken ribs from Wombat-man's last attack twinged and he dropped his three-eighths inch into the Hell portal.

He stood there staring into the swirling red and black liquid for a moment considering whether it was worth risking his hand for the chance to find his wrench.

No, I'll just expense it on the next report, he thought.

Kari knew how badly the heroes had beaten him up last time so she should be understanding. The Greatest Necromancer Who Ever Was or Will Be would never let him get away with it. but ever since The Greatest Necromancer Who Ever Was or Will Be had gotten big and bad enough to attract the notice of the Fairness League the Greatest Necromancer Who Ever Was or Will Be had decided that looking at expense reports was beneath her. Jim wasn't sure if he preferred it that way or not.

On one hand, he was making more money with better benefits and less direct oversight from a woman who would have made him stick his hand blindly into Hell rather than pay five dollars for a wrench. On the other hand, the new heroes that attacked broke a lot more of his bones.

He wished he could just find a different job, but once you had "evil goon" on your resume it was almost impossible to find work outside the Hench-person's Union. At least their hospital was free to use. He was pretty sure he had spent more of the last two years in one of their beds than out of one.

He was walking around to where the new guy, Carter, was working so he could ask to borrow his wrench when he first heard it. The telltale sign that a hero was attacking: the sound of untrained mainte-nance workers and administrative assistants being beaten senseless by martial arts masters.

Jim heaved a sigh. Maybe he would get lucky and it would be one of the "stealth" heroes. Maybe even that guy who thought if he put a cardboard box over himself no one would know he was there. If you pretended that you couldn't hear them they would usually leave you alone, so he kept walking like there weren't grunts and screams of pain coming from the other room.

Just as he was coming up to where Carter was kneeling next to another one of the portal stabilizers, the loud banging of a fully-grown man crawling through an air duct started to reverberate around the room.

Carter stood up and said, "Do you hear that?"

Before Jim could think, *you idiot*, a blur in red and blue slammed into the ground so hard that it threw Carter into the air. Liphistiidae-Lad jumped up and uppercut Carter in the jaw to flip him upside down before spinning midair to roundhouse kick him in the spine so hard that Jim could hear the snap.

The kick launched him out over the Hell portal and Jim watched in horror as a now unconscious Carter fell into the land of fire and brimstone.

Something broke inside Jim then. Carter hadn't even been there a month. He'd just gotten out of rehab and no one outside the supervillain world had been willing to give him a chance. He had taken the only option he had left, and now he was dead because this "hero" couldn't tell the difference between a bodyguard and a mechanic.

Jim knew he had to fight back or The Greatest Necromancer Who He Never Gave a Crap About would find out and kill him for insubordination, but he didn't care. All he could see was Carter's limp, broken body falling in slow motion through the portal to Hell.

"What is wrong with you?" Jim shouted.

Liphistiidea-Lad stopped mid-step and turned towards Jim. The break from generic "I'm gonna get you" and "stop right there" lines the hench-people used to keep up appearances must have caught him off guard.

A small, very scared voice told Jim he could still make a show of fighting back and hope he didn't get thrown into Hell too, but the much louder, much angrier part of him kept yelling instead.

"That guy had a daughter he was trying to get back to! He had a name, not that you care to know what it was! Did you even think before you round-house kicked him into Hell?! Did you for one second stop to think, 'maybe I don't need to break every single bone in this maintenance man's body to take him down' huh?! A light tap would do it for most of us! Heck you could just pretend to hit us and we would take the fall! You know not a single one of us 'goons' actually wants The Greatest Jerk Who Ever Was or Will Be to succeed, right?! No, you just see us all as little evil wretches who deserve as much mercy as you just showed Carter!"

As Jim's tirade came to an end and his spine had not been snapped in half like he had been expecting, he realized Liphistiidea-Lad was just standing there frozen, staring at him. Jim was breathing hard after all his shouting.

Why hadn't he been kicked to crap yet? He was even less armed than he usually was. He was a prime senseless beating target. As the moment stretched on and nothing happened Jim's glare glazed over. His anger was fading and the shock of what he had just done set in on him.

He was a dead man...

He was a dead man.

"How old is his daughter?"

Jim looked back up. Liphistiidea-Lad was holding his mask in his hand. Long blonde hair framed a chiseled, unreadable face as he looked down from the edge of the Hell portal.

"She just turned nine. He said her birthday gift was him finally getting clean."

For some reason that detail seemed like the most important thing in the world. The huge man in front of Jim took a deep breath, and then suddenly he was pressing something into Jim's hand.

"If I don't make it back, you have to take this down to level three. The demonic sigil that is sustaining this portal is directly below this room. Follow the instructions exactly and it will consecrate these grounds and close the portal forever." With that he turned back to the portal.

"Wait!" Jim yelled out, but Liphistiidea-Lad didn't. Instead he did a perfect swan dive into Hell.

Jim was left trying to process what had just happened. Did his fury actually get through to the man? Had he never stopped to look at who he was attacking to see that they were real people with real lives of their own? Jim had thought all those League members were just in it for the glory and the opportunity to legally beat people up, but this one hadn't hesitated to risk his life the moment he was told there was a good man he might be able to save.

There was very little chance that Liphistiidea-Lad

made it back from Hell, but if he told the other members of the League what Jim had said maybe they would take it easy on the little guys from now on. Maybe Jim had done some good while he sentenced himself to death. He had a revelation then.

He could do whatever he wanted and Sharron couldn't hurt him any more than she already would. He could call her Sharron instead of that stupid name she insisted on.

He felt the weight of fear fall off his shoulders, and he stood up straight for the first time he could remember. He looked down at the small bag he had been given, and he knew what he had to do.

He was a dead man, but at least he had done some good.

He was a dead man, but he could at least do a little more good.

He was a dead man, but he had never felt more alive.

Joshua Lorentson was born in Eldersburg, Maryland in 1998. He is an engineer with a deep rooted need for creative expression. Whether it be short stories, novels, or video games he enjoys writing in any format. His parent's introduced him to fantasy at a very young age with The Chronicles of Narnia by C. S. Lewis, and he has been in love with stories of all kinds ever since. Taking inspiration from classical books like The Lord of the Rings and modern works like Arcane, he enjoys intricate world building and creating deeply introspective characters to experience those worlds.

Image

Coming

Soon

The Year Skyler Richards Ruined Christmas

By Michael Barron

For decades, certain members of the Richards family would argue that their last holiday together was ruined because Skyler ate McDonald's on Christmas.

Technically, the troubles began years earlier, when Skyler's grandmother started kidnapping children and locking them in her basement.

However, as the sun set on that fateful December twenty-fifth, all Skyler's mother could do was sit on the curb across from the remains of her childhood home and think of how earlier that day her teenage daughter announced, "I'm getting McDonald's."

"What?" her mother asked while riding in the minivan's passenger seat.

"I said I'm getting McDonald's." Skyler pointed at the upcoming exit.

"It's Christmas," Mrs. Richards said. "You can't have McDonald's on Christmas."

"But I'm starving." Skyler took the exit.

"What's happening?" Skyler's father asked from the backseat.

"Skyler thinks she's stopping for McDonald's."

"But it's Christmas."

"That's what I told her. Skyler, is this a joke?"

"You don't want to ruin your appetite," her father said. "Grandma will have turkey, mashed potatoes, cranberry stuffing. . ."

"We're not eating for hours," said Skyler, who was an art major at Towson University and no longer accustomed to being told when to eat.

"What's happening?" Jake, Skyler's fifteen-year-old brother, pulled out his earbuds.

"Your sister is getting McDonald's," her mother said. "On Christmas."

"Oh." He put the earbuds back in.

"They might not even be open," Her mom said as Skyler pulled behind a row of cars in the drive-thru.

Fifteen minutes later, they were back on the highway. Skyler kept one hand on the wheel while drowning her Chicken McNuggets in the honey mustard packet balanced on her lap. Refusing to assist her daughter, Mrs. Richards rolled down her window so her mother wouldn't sniff out the scent of fried fat.

The late December wind transformed the minivan into a meat locker, but no one complained. Even Terry

Gross on NPR spoke in a hushed voice, as if afraid to catch Mrs. Richard's wrath.

The window was still down when they turned into Grandma's neighborhood, so they all heard the screams. It sounded like pleas for mercy.

"Good Lord," Skyler's father said. "Someone's having an unhappy Christmas."

Her mother tutted. "This town has changed. Another boy went missing last week. Probably addicted to drugs. But *none* of us will mention that. Do you understand?"

They were all still nodding when Skyler pulled up the gravel driveway. Grandma was waiting for them outside. She wore her red skirt and candy cane sweater, the same outfit she'd worn every Christmas since Jake was born. As they climbed out, she raised her arms, ready to embrace the whole world.

She hugged Jake first, followed by Skyler, Skyler's father and finally Skyler's mother, who cut the hug short to ask, "What happened to your arm?"

Grandma pulled down her sleeve, hiding the bandages covering her forearm. "If you must know, that darn cat is getting too big for her britches. She took a swipe at me just now. Can you believe that, Alice? On Christmas!"

They all gathered in the kitchen where everyone exclaimed how delicious the turkey smelled. Then they ventured into the living room to examine the mountains of presents surrounding the tree. "Don't touch any of those until after dinner," Grandma scolded with a smile.

They took their usual places around the house. Jake sat in the easy chair texting while the long-haired calico, Daisy, perched on the ottoman. Mr. Richards sat on the couch watching the Ravens lose to the Eagles. Skyler's mother lingered in the kitchen doorway, washing dishes whenever her mother turned her back. Skyler stood in the hallway, pulling books off the shelves. Most were crammed with scientific and historical misinformation. However, she enjoyed examining the illustrations while writing poetry in the margins.

They'd been going about their usual holiday routine for an hour when Mrs. Richards took Skyler's arm. "Ask the boys what they want to drink. We'll be. . . What's that?"

Skyler glanced at her white sleeve. The smallest drop of McDonald's honey mustard glared up at her like a furious yellow eye.

"Clean that up right now."

"How?"

"She keeps stain sticks in the laundry room. Do it now. If she sees that. . ." Skyler's mother glanced over her shoulder toward the kitchen. "I won't lie for you, Skyler. If she catches you, *you'll* have to tells her what you've done."

* * *

All Alice wanted for Christmas was for everything to go back to the way it used to be.

Skyler had been such a sweet baby. She would press her tiny face against Alice's cheek, and Alice would sing to her, keeping her safe. Then one day she turned around and that sweet baby had become a grown woman who decided she was an "artist" and interested in things she had never been interested in as a child.

As Skyler left to clean up her mess, Alice stepped back into the kitchen. "Is there anything I can—"

"Stay right there," her mother said. "I don't need you messing up my system."

Alice closed her eyes and took a deep breath. Before she could lose her nerve she said, "The Christmas tree is awfully close to the—"

"The Christmas tree is where it's always been."

"It's bone dry and inches from the fireplace. Let me—"

Her mother turned on the blender, silencing her with a roar that rattled the cabinets.

When she flipped it off, she said, "I hear Skyler is still living in that apartment. She should be home with you, not in some city. Keep your ducklings under your wing, Alice. This world is full of forces eager to seduce children like Skyler."

As her mother scolded her for the state of the world, Alice stared down the hall, toward the laundry room, where Skyler searched for a stain stick. Seeing her daughter in that room made her feel ill.

Of course her mother wouldn't complain about the apartment in front of Skyler. To the rest of the family she was a sweet old lady who baked the best Christmas cookies in the world. They got off easy. None of them knew what she was really like. That's why Alice had to do exactly what her mother wanted, otherwise she might turn to one of them and *everything* would come out.

But what scared Alice the most was how much she agreed with her mother. She wanted to keep her ducklings close. Staring down the hall, she pictured herself slamming the laundry room door and locking Skyler inside, keeping her safe until she was that sweet little baby again.

Skyler jiggled the laundry room closet's doorknob, but —as always—it was locked. She searched the cabinets, moving as silently as possible. This was the one part of the house they weren't allowed to enter. "You don't need to see that mess," Grandma would say, even though it was just as tidy as every other room.

The honey mustard shined like an emergency beacon. There was no doubt Grandma would spot it when Skyler passed the mashed potatoes. She would make a comment, and Skyler would have to reveal she'd stopped for McDonald's. Then grandma would say, "Oh, I'm sorry you didn't think I would have enough food," and Skyler's mother would stew in silence for the rest of the holidays.

Skyler needed this break. A week ago her roommate moved back to Seattle with three months' rent still left unpaid. Two days after that, her advisor had a "constructive" conversation with her, which amounted to, "maybe you should be a business major." An evil part of her agreed.

She wanted to tell her mother about all that, but she had long ago learned that the holidays were not the time to pile on more stress. She could tell grandma. However, bringing her real-world problems into her grandmother's house felt sacrilegious. This place was a sanctuary, a time capsule where nothing changed. And that purity would be tarnished if she didn't find a damn stain stick.

She stood on her tiptoes and groped behind the washer. She even tried the closet door again, but it was still locked. Of course that would be where she kept the cleaning supplies.

Creeping into the living room, Skyler asked her father, "Where does Grandma keep her keys?" She expected him to say he didn't know. Why would he? Instead he pointed at the side table by the Christmas tree.

"In the candy dish." He blinked awake, turning from the television. "What do you need them for?"

The honey mustard burned against Skyler's wrist as she snatched the keys. "Just helping Mom."

She made sure Grandma was still in the kitchen before creeping back to the laundry room. After some trial and error, she found the key that fit into the lock. It was only when she pulled the door open that she discovered it didn't lead to a closet at all.

* * *

All Jake wanted for Christmas was to be anywhere else.

"Who're you texting?" Jake's mom popped out of nowhere so suddenly, Daisy hopped off the ottoman.

"No one." He stuck the phone in his pocket.

"Is it Nikki? I've seen her around. She's very pretty."

Jake responded by heading for the guest bedroom, which had a door that locked. He wanted to bring Daisy with him, but the cat had wandered toward the laundry room. He wasn't going anywhere near that part of the house, not after what happened last year.

The previous Christmas had been just like every other Christmas in Jake's life. They'd opened presents at home, driven to Grandma's, ate dinner, opened more presents, ate dessert, and gone to bed. Everything was perfect–or at least following their usual routine–until Jake woke in the middle of the night with an unbearably swollen boner.

He'd tried to handle the situation in the bathroom, but he couldn't get in the right state of mind with the cold tiles against his ass and his grandparents' wedding photos staring at him from the counter. Who puts their wedding photos in the bathroom?

So he changed locations. He made himself comfortable in the laundry room, pulled up a trusty website and got to work.

Then his grandmother walked in.

There is no good time for a grandparent to walk in on their grandchild masturbating (scientific fact), but Jake's grandmother walked in at the absolute worst moment.

The writhing bodies on the 6.7-inch screen had been his whole universe. He was only vaguely aware of the door creaking open. Then his grandmother was there, staring dead-eyed. Jake's guts turned to icy mush. The world quivered and swelled, as if his brain was insisting this was all a dream and was trying to wake up. Far too late, he turned to hide himself, while grabbing a tissue to clean up the mess. The video kept playing, filling the tiny room with moans and wet grunts.

When he'd looked up again, she'd vanished. There was nothing for him to do but put the sugar cookie-scented lotion back in the bathroom and retreat to his air mattress, where he simmered in sweaty self-loathing.

He spent the rest of the holidays feeling like his world was on the verge of ending. While they ate chocolate chip waffles, packed leftovers, and watched Charlie Brown learn the meaning of Christmas, he braced himself for the moment his grandmother would say, "By the way, I caught your sweet baby boy pleasuring himself in my laundry room, and you wouldn't believe what the people in the video he was watching were doing with inflatable pool toys."

But it never came.

Jake was so blinded by shame, it wasn't until after New Years that he wondered what his grandmother was doing up at three in the morning in the first place. Also, why had she entered the laundry room from the closet?

* * *

The room at the bottom of the stairs desperately wanted to be cheerful. The rug was the color of fresh spring grass. Nickelodeon-orange sofas furnished the space along with artificial trees and flowers. The ceiling was painted sky blue. However, Skyler still felt the cold cement through the rug.

Did her mother know this room existed? She had to. She'd grown up in this house. Maybe it was a bomb shelter. A massive row of storage shelves ran along one wall, holding enough supplies to last three apocalypses. There was bottled water, canned vegetables, canned meat, laundry detergent, and a bulk supply of....

"Gotcha!" She snatched one of the countless stain sticks off the lowest shelf and got to work scrubbing out the honey mustard.

It wasn't until she was standing still, allowing the cleaner to seep in, that she heard the sobbing. Skyler turned. There was no one with her in the room. She checked behind a sofa, but all she found were boxes filled with old *Archie* and *Disney* comics.

Maybe her mom was crying because Skyler ate McDonald's on Christmas.

The crying became louder the closer she approached the shelves. Holding her breath, she pushed some cans aside and leaned in toward the whitewashed plywood forming the back of the shelves. Now she was positive the sobs were coming from the other side. She could even hear voices shushing someone to be quiet.

Skyler stepped back, knocking a can to the floor with a dull *thunk*.

The voices grew silent.

Skyler pictured herself running upstairs and joining the others, enjoying the turkey and the presents, forgetting this impossible room existed. However, instead, she peeked behind the shelves. A row of padlocks fastened the massive piece of furniture in place. She stood frozen, staring at the locks, not moving until the crying began again.

All Bryan wanted for Christmas was time away from his family.

He knew that was harsh. He loved Alice and the kids, but working customer service in a financial call center was stressful and being a parent doubly so.

At least he had his sanctuary.

It wouldn't be long now. Soon they would eat dinner, open presents, gobble down dessert, and then Christmas will be over. They'll push the table back, inflate the air mattresses for the kids and one by one go to bed. He'd lay awake, though, waiting until he was positive everyone was asleep. Then he'd swipe the keys from the candy dish and unlock the door in the laundry room. That's when his *real* vacation would begin.

He'd found his sanctuary nine years earlier. Skyler and Jake were still kids, screaming, running around, breaking things. Alice was so stressed about visiting her mother she kept snapping at everyone, except her mother. On top of all this, Bryan had the Everest of headaches.

He'd scoured the house for ibuprofen, the only thing that ever cut through the pain. All the bathroom had to offer was expired baby aspirin. He might as well take sugar pills.

His wife and her mother were in the kitchen having a debate he didn't want to get roped into, so he swiped the keys from the candy dish and went to see if the laundry room closet had any pain killers. He was so desperate, he didn't even ask for permission.

It was only after he unlocked the door that he realized the "closet" was in fact a flight of stairs, and at the bottom of those stairs was something even better than ibuprofen: comic books.

Bryan adored comics as a kid. Never *Tales From the Crypt* or *The Punisher*. Nothing violent or scary. What he loved were *Duck Tales*, *Flintstones*, *Casper*, and *Archie*. That basement had them all. It was a family-friendly comic book Narnia.

He considered mentioning the basement to his wife, but admitting he had never noticed a room in his mother-in-law's house was beyond humiliating.

However, during every visit since then, after everyone else went to bed, he'd grab the keys, sneak downstairs and stay up until one in the morning reading comics. Of course the room wasn't perfect. The walls occasionally made noises that sounded like crying or moaning. Once he even thought he heard pleading. But that was just old pipes. Houses made all sorts of noises that were easy to ignore once you got used to them.

After the final padlock clattered to the floor, a silence fell over the basement. Whoever had been crying was now quiet. Maybe it was her imagination.

Skyler leaned against the shelves and pushed. It was only then that she realized they were on wheels and slid aside with barely any effort, revealing a doorway.

Darkness shrouded the room. The only light came from a television displaying Bugs Bunny hitting Elmer Fudd with a mallet. The TV was so bright and the shadows so deep a moment passed before she noticed the six children staring at her.

She stepped back, too shocked to make a sound.

Her initial thought was they were ghosts. The frail, hollow-eyed children looked more like memories than actual people. The small crowd huddled around a sofa, clutching one another. They appeared to range in age from pre-school to early teens, but the light was so dim, and their faces covered in so many bruises, it was impossible to be certain.

The children's clothes were pristine, though. Every button-down shirt, every blouse, every pair of slacks were neatly ironed. She recognized the clothing from family photos. One girl wore the same red dress Skyler's mother wore when she won the county spelling bee. The smallest child–whose bloodshot eyes revealed they were the one crying–wore the lamb costume Jake wore during his kindergarten Christmas pageant.

Skyler stared at the children, heart pounding so hard she could barely stand.

The tallest of the kids, a girl in a pair of Skyler's old overalls, stepped forward. "Please—"

Skyler shut the door, locking it.

* * *

Lightning (now called Daisy) was a cat and therefore possessed no concept of Christmas. However, if she had, all she would want was her Casey back.

Lightning knew Casey's name. The other food givers in their household called that name whenever she returned home. Then Lightning would meow and brush against her leg, asking for pets. Casey was Lightning's girl. She had a soft voice and gentle hands. She held Lightning during thunderstorms and fed her from the table.

Then came the day Casey carried Lightning into the backyard. Lightning was staring at the birds and leaves, taking in the sounds and smells. She was so caught up she didn't hear the footsteps until rough hands snatched her and Casey.

They dragged them both into a car–which Lightning only knew from visits to the vet–and threw them inside. Yowling and hissing, Lightning scratched at the seats, until a harsh voice barked at them. It was only when Casey stopped screaming and was holding Lightning close to her pounding heart that the voice turned gentle.

Lightning was a cat and therefore possessed little concept of the English language. However, if she had, she'd know the voice said, "You're not safe out here. It's dangerous. I'll take care of you, the way I should have cared for my own family."

Daisy's white fangs ripped into the scraps of turkey Jake offered under the table, tearing and devouring the flesh. Skyler had no idea how long she'd been watching. Christmas dinner was spread before her; casseroles, muffins, ham, fruit salad, three different styles of potatoes and a turkey the size of a honey-roasted toddler.

"Skyler." Her mother passed her a bowl of stuffing.

Skyler took it. The stuffing was the color of the bruises covering the children's faces.

She dumped a glob beside the slices of turkey and casserole on her plate. How had she gotten here?

The Christmas tree loomed behind her,

surrounded by presents. Flames cracked in the fire-place. A woman on TV knocked on a door. There had been knocking as she ran up the stairs. The kids behind the wall were pounding on the shelves, shouting at her to....

"Would you like some potatoes?" Her mother asked.

Skyler took the offered food.

"Thank you for taking care of that," her mother whispered, nodding to her sleeve, which was now one hundred percent stain-free.

Skyler nodded. The flames in the fireplace crackled.

"I don't know about the rest of you...." Grandma grinned. "But I can't wait to open my presents. Tell me Jake, were you a good boy this year?"

Jake shrugged.

"I bet you were."

"I guess." He gnawed on his turkey.

"Well, I suppose we'll find out when we see what Santa brought. There's one extra big present over there that just might be—"

Skyler opened her mouth and puked all over her Christmas dinner.

"Skyler!" her mom shouted.

Heaving, Skyler spewed half-digested Chicken McNuggets and fries, putting them on full display for the world to see. She was aware of her father covering his mouth, as if he were going to be sick and her grandma reaching for the napkins, but they were all miles away.

All she could mutter was, "I'm sorry," before bolting for the bathroom.

Kneeling on the tiles, she shut her eyes and leaned over the toilet. Her stomach rolled as she gagged and spat, her McDonald's vomit breath wafting off the water.

Someone tapped on the door. "Skyler?" It was Jake.

"Yeah?" She groaned.

"Mom says this wouldn't have happened if you hadn't eaten you-know-what."

"Thanks."

"Are you okay?"

"No." She grabbed some toilet paper and wiped her mouth. "Come in."

"You're not taking a shit are you?"

"I wouldn't be telling you to come in if I was."

Jake cracked the door and peeked inside.

Gripping the counter, Skyler pulled herself up. "Grandma's done something really bad."

"What?" He didn't mean, "What did she do?" He appeared to not comprehend the statement.

"Follow me." She staggered past him, leading the way down the hall.

"I'm not going in there." He stopped outside the laundry room.

"Why not?"

He took two steps back but lingered close enough to watch her pick the keys off the floor, where she must have dropped them. Jake whispered a curse as she opened the door, revealing the impossible staircase.

He didn't catch up until she was at the bottom of the steps. "Grandma has a basement?"

"That's not all." Clutching her stomach, Skyler stuck the keys into the padlock. "I need to show you something. It's kind of...." She still hadn't found the right adjective by the time the final padlock clattered to the floor.

During the seconds it took to push the shelves aside, she convinced herself she would only see a bare wall. Maybe she'd been hallucinating. Maybe the chemicals they used to process McNuggets were rotting her brain. That wouldn't be so bad.

But the chamber was still there. So were the children.

"Please," The girl in Skyler's overalls said. "We—"

"The fuck?" Jake pushed the shelves back into place. He grabbed the padlocks and started fastening them. "Who are those people?"

"I don't know. Grandma's keeping them in there." She shook her head at the absurdity of that statement. "We need to let them out. Right?"

Even as she spoke, she saw her grandmother–who always baked them brownies and contributed to church food drives–being interrogated by the police in a small, windowless room. Skyler's mother would never forgive her.

"Maybe they deserve to be in there," Jake said. "Or maybe Grandma doesn't know about them."

"Your grandma knows," the overalls girl called from behind the shelf.

Jake opened his mouth, but before he could offer a rebuttal, she shouted, "My name's Casey Price. I've been down here for five years. My dads probably think I'm dead. You have to help us. Just give me a phone. I'll...."

A sharp ringing filled Skyler's ears, as if her brain was censoring what she was hearing. But it was too late. Her feet were already pushing her forward and her hands were already turning the keys in the padlocks. She expected Jake to stop her, she wanted him to, but he remained frozen even as the final padlock fell to the floor and she pushed the shelves aside.

Even with their prison wide open, the kids remained in darkness, as if anticipating the shelves to snap back into place. A moment ago, Casey had been begging to get back to her dads. Now she drew away from the light, bumping into a boy wearing Jake's old blue blazer.

Skyler willed the prisoners to change their minds and remain in the chamber so she and her brother could return to Christmas dinner.

"Skyler!" They all jumped as her mom called. "Grandma's asking for you and Jake."

As if the voice had woken her, Casey stepped forward. The boy in the blazer picked up the child in the lamb costume and followed. Then came the rest. As they crossed the threshold, Skyler and Jake stepped back, allowing them to pass.

Casey led the way. At first they crept up the steps, as though expecting an invisible wall to come crashing down. However, as they ascended they picked up speed, until they were sprinting.

Skyler and Jake were still in the basement when the screaming began. It sounded as though every member of the Richards family dating all the way back to their great, great, great grandfather who'd immigrated from Wales were shrieking at once. Through it all, her grandmother shouted, "Stop them! These children keep breaking into my house to rob me!"

Skyler and Jake bolted up the stairs, through the laundry room, down the hall and into an erupting volcano that used to be the living room. Someone had knocked the Christmas tree into the fireplace. Cranberry sauce and gravy splattered the carpet. All the adults were on their feet while frail, bruised children ran about struggling with the windows and door, which Grandma always kept locked.

"Stop them!" Skyler's grandmother screamed. "Bryan! Do something!"

Trying to be a good guest, Skyler's father grabbed the child in the lamb outfit. "I got one! Now what do I —" The girl in the spelling bee dress punched him in the gut.

The only person who didn't move was Skyler's mother. She stood stock still, clutching her napkin until Casey flung the candy dish at her face.

"Asshole! I heard you talking about us. You knew, and you didn't do anything."

"Mom?" Skyler shouted.

She and her mother locked eyes, but before either could say a word, an eardrum-piercing shriek filled the house. The fire alarm was going off.

Skyler had been so distracted by her world falling apart, she hadn't noticed the flames spreading up the bone-dry Christmas tree, transforming it into an indoor bonfire. Presents burned while fire climbed the curtains and wallpaper.

"Everybody out!" Skyler rushed across the living room, slipping on the cranberry sauce as she went. Using the keys to unlock the front door, she flung it wide open. The children ran after her, out into the fresh December air.

* * *

All Skyler had wanted for Christmas was to get through the holidays with minimal drama. Now, she sat on the curb across the street, watching her grandmother's house burn to the ground. Somehow, she could still smell the turkey.

Frail children wandered the neighborhood, keeping their distance from Skyler's family, who watched as the police and fire trucks pulled up. Her grandmother was already shouting at the officers about how a band of "hoodlums" broke into her house and set her tree on fire.

Casey clutched Daisy–who she kept calling "Lightning"–while Jake held his phone to her ear so she could talk to her dads. Skyler wanted to walk over to them but didn't have the strength to stand.

"Skyler?" She hadn't heard her mother approaching until she sat beside her.

"You knew," Skyler tore at a clump of dead grass.

"I didn't approve," her mother said. "I tried to convince her not to but.... She's done so much for this family, and I wasn't the best daughter.... And the first couple kids really did come from horrible families.... And I told her not to keep those keys in that candy dish, anyone could pick them up, but she never listens..... And you have to understand she came from a different generation. Back then...."

Skyler stood to walk away.

"Skyler!" Her mother grabbed her arm. "I know you're upset, but you should know that before...." She motioned to the flames and paramedics collecting children. "...all this happened, I came clean to your grandmother. I told her you ate McDonald's for lunch. And while I still don't approve, she said she was fine with it." She wiped her eyes. "All she cared about was that you weren't hungry. It just goes to show what a special person she really is."

Michael Barron's fiction has been published by "Graveside Press" "NewMyths.com" and "Uncharted Magazine." You can find him at http://michaelbarronauthor.com and @barronauthor.bsky.social on Bluesky. Michael is a member of the neurodivergent community, and his experiences inspire his writing.

When he is not writing or reading he is either training for a marathon with his wife or working as a librarian at the Baltimore County Public Library, where he leads creative writing programs. He has undertaken a never-ending quest for the world's greatest hot sauce.

Self-Taxidermy:
Dressed to

Kill

by C. Piveral

Self-Taxidermy: Dressed to Kill

By C. Piveral

1. Freeze until ready. It's important to keep the body from spoiling before you begin the process of preserving. Start young, before signs of aging occur.

2. Acquire the necessary materials:

- Sharp knife
- Sewing needle
- Thread
- Borax, Alcohol, or your preferred preserving agent (Retinol / Niacinamide / Hyaluronic acid)
- Stuffing (Juvéderm / Restylane / Collagen / Silicone / Fat Graft)

3. Prepare the form. Again, start preservation as

early as possible. It helps to have a guide or example from which to work—society recommends Gal Gadot, Bella Hadid, Jenna Ortega, or others. Never mind that they're much younger, and richer. We don't care where the project starts only where it ends. One must be hard in order to achieve the recommended softness.

4. Remove the skin. Carefully slice a seam up the belly. Be careful not to puncture the body cavity or any organs, which could mar the skin. Loosen the flesh by sliding the knife between skin, muscle, and viscera. Peel back the flesh. Strip away as much fat as possible. If it helps you can think of it like removing clothing—dowdy and outdated today becomes your fashionable body of tomorrow.

5. Remove the unnecessary. Remove the parts that spoil the illusion of perfection. Remove the parts that smell bad. Remove as much excess flesh as possible, the less of you that remains the better.

6. Smooth the form with sandpaper or a small knife such as a scalpel. Perfect the shape as a scaffold for more smooth, youthful skin. Don't overthink the details, the exterior view is what's most important.

7. Hollow out the head—you'll need to remove your brain, eyes, and tongue. Even when you speak less, you speak too much—better to be seen and not heard. It will take patience and a strong stomach. Remain committed.

8. Hide, in a cold, dark place (like familial expectations, the board room, or a popular dating site). Let the viscous hide dry. Place the carcass, flesh-side down, inside a box on a generous coating of self-loathing. Monitor it so that it doesn't become difficult to mold. Keep it in the back of the closet lest your disassembled-self offend.

9. Soak the skin. When you have toughened up, hydrate again. Lysol disinfectant and table salt help exorcise thoughts of autonomy and may mask the pungent smell of hematic tang. Hydrate, hydrate, hydrate—not for comfort, not for organ function, not to fight impaired brain function—hydrated skin is plump and youthful.

10. Hyde. Use a pickling agent at this point to stem further weeping, making sure to remove any sticky bits of flesh or fat. *This is a good time to refer to earlier examples of good form, or perhaps Marilyn Monroe, Jayne Mansfield, or Jennifer Lopez (the much younger version, certainly not the current woman).

11. Dress your form. Stuffing the hide is as easy as dressing a doll. When fixing the preserved skin onto the new form, carefully smooth out any irregularities or unnatural lumps. Note: Here, flaws such as aging, genetic variation, metabolic differences, and differing cultural beauty standards, are considered outside the standard of "natural."

12. Sew it shut. Stitch the original cut with as tight and invisible a suture as possible. Scars, while signs of a lived life, are unsightly and may spoil the appearance of the final product.

13. Display your new self. While traditional taxidermy might bare the animal's teeth, it's best not to threaten. We suggest a more demure but alluring position that invites attention on other's terms. Arrange a *tasteful* tableau of heels and exposed skin. If you choose to display a more trad-wife, stay immortalized in a domestic position baking bread or cleaning baseboards. Smile.

14. Care for your work. Don't let your efforts go to waste—dampness from too many tears can result in mildew, while excessive dryness (aging) can cause hides to crack and split. If the form settles, in an unpleasant way, consider splitting it open and restructuring again, and again, and again. Your preoccupation is perfection!

* * *

C. Piveral is a speculative fiction writer whose stories combine the dark and whimsical. Her short fiction has appeared in magazines and anthologies such as

Flame Tree Press's "Robots & Artificial Intelligence", "Apparition Lit", Common Deer Press's "Short Tails", and more. A transplant from the American Midwest, she now lives near the Colorado mountains with her rescue dog, Ziggy. For more of her work, visit her website at www.cpiveral.com.

Image
Coming
Soon

The Demon Box

By Jeanette Gibson

Lily gently removed the loose brick and felt inside the hole for the hidden key. Thank goodness, she thought (assuming goodness existed), that she had tended the shop a couple times for Chloe.

Her hand trembled. Thievery, deceit, dishonesty of any kind had been unthinkable to Lily since she was old enough to comprehend the difference between right and wrong, good and bad, salvation and damnation, and the consequences of the wrong choice: beatings and two days in a dark closet, with no food and a bucket for a toilet.

Lily's foster parents had taken her on as a divine test of their faith. Transforming a sinful, willful creature into a pure vessel worthy of receiving god's grace, they believed, would shower blessings all around. The day came, at last, when she aged out of the foster care system and set out on her own.

Lily held the key tightly in her hand. It almost burned with the heat of her guilt. Her breath quickened and she began to perspire.

"Remember!" she whispered to herself. "Remember why you're here and do what you have to!"

* * *

She forced herself to replay in her mind the way Rachel had treated her almost from the time she moved in. Lily was excited about living with a roommate her age and having a friend—her first real friend.

Rachel was "cool." She was pretty, vivacious, popular and, Lily soon found out, manipulative. Their fun, shared times together became less and less frequent, until it dawned on Lily that she meant nothing more to Rachel than half the rent...and a source of amusement.

When friends came over or when they went to parties, Rachel made Lily perform like a trained monkey. One time, Rachel raved about Lily's excellent dancing, then cued everyone to abandon her in the middle of the floor so they could mock her awkwardness.

They teased her mercilessly about her virginity, something Lily had only a vague idea about. Most humiliating was a date she had with Kurt, one of

Rachel's boyfriends. He took her back to his place after a burger at McDonald's. As soon as they were inside, he pressed her to the wall and began to kiss and grope her. Lily, who hardly had been touched at all during her young life, didn't resist at first. The sensations were too intoxicating.

All of a sudden, her eyes opened wide, and she pushed Kurt away. "I'm feeling funny. It might be a baby starting!"

It was true fear Kurt saw on Lily's face. He overcame the urge to laugh and continued nonchalantly, "Oh, no, it can't be that. Here's what you need to make a baby." Kurt unzipped his trousers and showed her.

Lily recoiled in disgust. "You can't make a baby with pee!"

Kurt struggled to stifle his laughter. He zipped up and turned back to face Lily.

"Jesus Christ, you are pathetic! Ha, ha, hooo-ee! Come on, now, I'll show you how it's done." Kurt motioned toward the bedroom.

Lily waved her hands in the air like a frustrated child. "No! No! I don't want a baby! Just take me home!"

Despite Rachel's probing, Lily wouldn't say a word about her date with Kurt. Lily went to bed early and lay awake staring into the dark until she drifted off.

* * *

The next night, Rachel dragged a reluctant Lily to another party. "You don't want to miss this one, hon," Rachel said sweetly, touching her cheek to Lily's.

The usual gang was there, including Kurt. He brought drinks over to Rachel and Lily. After some small talk, he called out, "Hey, guys, come over here! Got something you'll wanna see!"

The noisy, mostly drunk group congregated around the computer, at which Kurt was seated. He inserted a flash drive and Lily's shy face popped onto the screen. Lowering her eyes, she said, "Hi, Kurt. I didn't think you'd show up."

What wasn't possible to capture on video of the previous night's date was recorded with audio. Kurt's candid camera escapade was a hit. Everyone hooted and hollered, made lewd comments, slapped Kurt on the back. Rachel laughed so hard black mascara tears rolled down her cheeks.

Everyone agreed it was "the best joke—the best show ever."

They poked at Lily and mocked her until her face was flooded with tears, as well; hot, angry tears. Anger not only at her tormentors, but also at herself, her foster parents, their religion. . . the world.

Lily screamed. The party people watched in stunned silence as she bolted out the door, into the enveloping, comforting void of night.

* * *

Lily remembered getting on a bus, riding for a long time, then getting off somewhere deep in the city's industrial guts. She recalled only brief flashes of the time she spend there—men sleeping in cardboard boxes; drunken, brawling voices; frightened faces—frightened *of her*.

Three days later, she found herself back at the apartment. Rachel startled when she opened the door.

"You!?" Rachel gave Lily a shriveling look. "Never thought I'd see you again! And you look like hell!"

Lily said nothing, just made a move to enter. Rachel stayed put, glaring defiantly.

"I came to get my stuff," Lily asserted.

"Your stuff? You freak out at the party, disappear for three days, and. . ."

Lily interrupted and took a step into the doorway. "You weren't worried? You didn't call anyone?"

Rachel had never seen Lily on the offensive and it rattled her. "Well!" she sneered. "You're supposed to be a big girl, even if you don't know a dick from a door knob!"

Rachel was shocked when, instead of cowering in shame, Lily forced her way in and shouted, "I need my clothes! What did you do with them?!"

Rachel wavered and backed off. "I. . . I don't have 'em. I thought you were gone for good, so I got rid of everything."

Lily grabbed Rachel's throat with a grimy hand. Her eyes were black cinders. "What did you do with my stuff?"

"Okay!" Stop!" Rachel croaked.

Lily released her grip.

"Holy fuck. Are you crazy?" Rachel rubbed her throat and coughed. "I took all your shit to Chloe's thrift shop."

* * *

"You're so stupid; so damn stupid!" Lily reproached herself, unable to believe she still felt compunctions about breaking in after the way she'd been treated.

The key turned easily in the lock, and there was no alarm to worry about. The odor of perspiration and musty years greeted her as she entered and looked around. Nothing of hers could be found, and she had nothing to wear but clothes on her back. She didn't want to steal, but. . .

"Maybe they haven't been put out yet." She went to the back of the shop, which served as office and sorting area. Bingo! Her things, mixed in with some others, were laid out, ready to be tagged. She stuffed them in a bag and sighed with relief.

Satisfied with her mission, Lily was about to leave when an uneasy feeling stopped her in her tracks. She retraced her steps, making sure nothing was out of place. Everything was fine. On the way to the back door she hesitated again, in front of the bookshelves. She wasn't much of a reader, but something compelled her to peruse the ragged volumes. There were the usual mystery novels, cookbooks, self-improvement guides. . . boring. . .

It felt as if a cold hand grabbed her, rooting her to

the spot. Her field of vision seemed to narrow, excluding everything but a thick, leather-bound volume jammed in the corner of the top shelf. Gold letters on the spine read, *Grimoire of Malediction.*

Without realizing what she was doing, Lily put the volume in her bag and made her way out, carefully locking the door behind her and returning the key to its hiding place.

She walked alone in the night, unafraid. It was as if a veil of protection surrounded her and some inexorable purpose guided her steps. Clearly, something deep inside her was changing.

After an hour's trek, Lily found herself back in the seedy neighborhood of her three lost days. She found a place where the little money she had got her a hole in the wall with a bed and a hotplate. It was a start.

She emptied the bags containing her possessions onto the bed, and the book, which she had forgotten about, tumbled out. Lily ran her fingers over the pebbled texture of the leather cover and the impressions of the gilded letters. It felt luxurious. . . seductive. Touching it sent a strange energy through her body. *It must be power*, she thought. *Happiness, even*? She laughed and opened the *Grimoire of Malediction*.

It was very old, hand written in antiquated English. The text was copiously illustrated with colored ink drawings of demons, and what Lily later learned were majick squares, alchemical formulas, and rituals. All the instructions had a single purpose: to exact vengeance on one's enemies or malefactors. The curses themselves were varied as a gourmet's recipe book. The most challenging and effective, and the one that appealed most to Lily, was the "demon box."

Lily was surprised by the amount of study and preparation required to construct the demon box. She would need time, and some of the exotic materials were fairly expensive. Lily took the least demanding job she could find—one that was unsupervised and would allow enough down time to study the grimoire. The job of parking lot attendant suited her needs perfectly.

Her studies progressed rapidly. The obvious fact that they involved dark forces was of no concern. The vessel her foster parents had prepared to receive god's grace instead had become devoid of anything holy or humane—the type of vacuum to which evil forces are naturally attracted. It was as if Lily had become *Lilith*.

It took two months to construct the demon box. The physical box was a seven-inch cube. Lily had meticulously followed the instructions for painting the sigils and symbols on the exterior, in the colors specified by the grimoire. One side was to be a "mirror to reflect the visage of the cursed one, that also is visible to the Daemon Resident." After puzzling for a long time, Lily came to the conclusion that a two-way mirror, like the ones used in police interrogation rooms, might fill the bill. It was difficult and expensive, but she managed to acquire a two-way mirror cut to fit one side of the box.

All that was left was to invoke the demon of malediction into the box. At the end of the ritual, she read aloud the final instruction:

Take me to where your enemy be,
Mirror his image for daemon to see.
As for the punishment,
Leave it to me.

* * *

Rachel gasped when she opened the door of her apartment to find a smiling, confident Lily standing there. Again.

"Go away!" she snapped and tried to slam the door shut.

Lily caught it and pushed it open.

"Hey, Rache," she said, "still lookin' for thrills?" Then in a less ominous tone, "I've got something you wouldn't bee-lieeve! Like, to die for! It's the most snatched thing ever-r."

Rachel wrinkled her nose and stared inquisitively at Lily. "Yeah? What is it?"

Lily giggled conspiratorially and sashayed into the room. "Come over here," she said with a big smile.

Rachel stood in front of her visitor, crossed her arms and scowled. "This better be good."

Lily took the box from her backpack, unwrapped it and held it up, mirror side facing Rachel.

"What is it, some sort of camera?"

"Well. . . kinda," Lily answered." She placed the box on the floor, stepped back and uttered the incantation: *Daemonium maledictionis, facere voluntatem tuam.*

The demon box glowed and emitted a sound like wind whistling through a tunnel.

Immediately, Rachel began to scratch herself. "What the hell is itching me?" She scratched harder, all over her body. "Ah! Ow-w! It's really bad, really bad! Did you do something to me?"

Lily shrugged and looked on in fascination.

Rachel's frantic scratching was starting to draw blood.

"What's happening?! It's getting worse—I can't stop! Help me!" she pleaded.

Lily answered in a quiet, composed voice. "I kind of think it's. . . too late, Rachel."

Rachel moaned and cried as the infernal itching intensified. Suddenly, instead of abrasions, her scratching produced clean little slices that oozed tiny droplets of blood. She didn't notice the change at first; sharp cuts don't always hurt right away.

When Rachel did notice, she couldn't stop scratching, even though her fingernails had transformed into razor-like blades that lacerated her body from head to toe. She stared in horror and disbelief as the blades grew longer. She screamed only once. A single "scratch" to the throat severed her vocal chords, ensuring the rest of her ordeal would be endured in silence.

The thirsty blades went on slicing and stabbing, until Rachel fell lifeless into a pool of jugular blood.

"Wow. It works," Lily observed dispassionately.

She wrapped the demon box in a square of black silk and stuffed it in her backpack. It was time to pay Kurt a visit.

* * *

The lights were on at Kurt's, and it appeared he had no company.

Lily rang the bell and stepped aside, so she wouldn't be seen if Kurt looked out the window.

When Kurt finally opened the door, Lily popped out. "Surprise! It's me!" she announced cheerily.

"Oh. . . ha, ha. . . you're Rachel's roommate, ha, ha. Sure I remember you. What's your name?"

"Lily," she said sternly. "My name is Lily."

"Oh, yeah, sure." Still chuckling, Kurt wolfishly looked her up and down. "So what can I do for you. . . *Lily*?"

Lily replied coquettishly. "Aren't you going to invite me in?"

"Well, *excusez-moi!*" Kurt answered. He half blocked the doorway so that Lily would have to brush against him. Lily pressed against his body more firmly than necessary to get past.

"Ooh, ha, ha, nice vibe, babe."

"Good," Lily teased.

"Like I said," Kurt continued in his mocking tone, "What, uh. . . do you want to pick up where we left off? Still need to take care of that nagging virgin problem?" He doubled over laughing.

"Ah-h. . . wel-l-l," Lily breathed seductively. "Actually, Kurt, I have something to show you. I showed it to Rachel and she just went to pieces over it. She wants you to see it, then. . ." She fingered the buttons on her blouse and grinned sheepishly at Kurt.

"Since you put it *that* way," he said still laughing. "Okay! Let's go!"

Lily unwrapped the demon box, held it out to Kurt and placed it on the floor in front of him. *Daemonium maledictionis, facere voluntatem tuam*, she intoned.

As before, the box lit up, and the small hurricane whistled inside.

"What is this shit" Kurt scoffed. His sneer became a belly laugh, which expanded into sobs of hysterical laughter. He bent over, holding his sides. "This is. . . ha, ha. . . the dumbest. . ."

In an instant, his mood changed to fear as he lost control and fits of convulsive laughter seized his body. The corners of his mouth stretched upward, in a freakishly wide grin. The mask-like rictus never left his face. "Can't breathe. . . can't breathe. . ." he managed to rasp faintly.

Kurt's face was livid, and his eyeballs protruded from their sockets. Relentless waves of demonic laughter conjoined hideously with shrieks of agony, punctuated now and then by the snap and crunch of breaking bone and sinew.

Lily propped her head on her hand and watched Kurt flail about like a demented marionette. "Easy, Kurt, you'll bust a gut," she warned.

At the end, Kurt's body jerked so violently his feet left the floor. His chest heaved unnaturally, and with a final grotesque guffaw, he lurched forward and collapsed. A crescent of rib poked out of his chest, and a bright red froth bubbled from his mouth.

"Must be a punctured lung," Lily observed.

Lily breathed in the damp night air. The darkness seemed to flow through her, becoming one with her. She felt strong. Protected.

Lily would have preferred to walk to her next destination. There would be no danger in doing so, even though strange men did accost her during her late-night ramblings. But after one look at her face under a streetlight, they retreated like banished ghosts.

The grimoire was adamant that the demon box be used only during the dark of the moon and before the first ray of sunlight. Reluctantly, Lily flagged down a cab. She had a friendly chat with the driver, gave him a generous tip and stepped out into the chill pre-dawn.

Lily mused as she walked up to the house of her former foster parents. The demon box seemed to mete out punishment that was somehow appropriate.

What will it cook up for these holy hypocrites? she wondered. *Whatever it is, it'll be the best joke—the best show ever!*

* * *

For most of her life Jeanette made a living as a freelance writer—mostly marketing communications and corporate collateral. She has also worked as a high-school French teacher, public relations coordinator, educational AV editor, and marketer of her and her husband's photography business.

Published:

"Qliphoth," Eidetic Magazine

"Coffin Bell," Madame Gray's Poe-Pourri of Terror (anthology)

"March Hag," Star*Line Poetry

"The Peregrinations of a Nascent Thought," Bullshit Magazine

Confession
to the Editor

by Jeff Stone

Confession to the Editor

By Jeff Stone

It didn't start innocently. I saw something on a picnic table in a stranger's driveway that I wanted but didn't have enough money for. So I took it. Aside from a pack of gum in a 7-11 when I was thirteen, this was my first theft. An aberration, or so I thought.

It was a Christmas stocking covered with images of a K-Pop band that I quickly stuffed into my jacket as the homeowner turned her back to talk to another neighbor. I did what I thought good thieves would do in this situation: I did not scamper off but instead asked a couple of questions about another item before walking probably too slowly to my Subaru. I may have sashayed.

I gave the stocking to my seven-year-old niece as a birthday present, then began scouring Facebook for future opportunities. Once you get going, you learn what neighborhoods are the safest to ply the trade — mainly comprised of steady middle-class families who really don't know what they have of value and are merely hoping to sell enough stuff to buy dinner at Outback with the profits.

Being a thin, middle-aged "mom-type," I wore baggy clothes with large pockets. I became adept at asking questions that often required the assistance of another family member who may be inside the house or in the backyard, offering windows of alone time to snatch a time-worn watch or set of steak knives.

My husband did notice from time to time the various trinkets and trash that I brought in, but during football season, our communication leveled off. He merely looked at our dining room table strewn with booklights, small chipped frames, and romance novels and grunted on his way to another beer from the mini-fridge he still has from the college he never graduated from. Sometimes, I threw out items within days of pilfering them — the thrill of the heist became more the point.

It was going along so smoothly until that fateful heavy knock on the door just after arriving home from a slew of "wins" at a crosstown neighborhood-wide yard sale.

I was cataloging my cache of items in the front room — an array of passable costume jewelry, a handsome scarf for my dad, a Captain & Tenille Greatest Hits CD because why not, and the garment that became the neuse around my neck . . . a hooded Columbia windbreaker which possessed within one of its pockets a lost set of earbuds. Earbuds that were tracked with an Apple AirTag and, therefore, traceable to my home.

After being delivered to a clean jail by a handsome police officer, I decided to represent myself — a costly mistake meant to save money. And here I sit, my home emptied of purloined treasures, five days into a two-week stint of house arrest. A three-year probation dictates I'm not to step within a thousand feet of a yard sale, flea market, or farmer's market . . . with perhaps the thought I might graduate to the thievery of local produce.

So, why am I writing to you, dear Editor? Why might the Gazette want to share my misanthropic ways and means with its readers? For one reason alone — I have an uncontrollable urge to violate my probation.

I'm making a comeback. I want my victims to be on high alert, as I want the best they've got. I would never have been caught if not for that stupid kid's earbuds and her sneaky mother.

And you won't see me coming, for I'm *not* actually a thin, middle-aged "mom-type" wearing baggy clothes. I'm someone altogether different. I might even be your neighbor.

* * *

Jeff Stone lives among the Blue Ridge Mountains of Virginia in a rapidly emptying nest. His spaniel, Dougie, has assured him he'll never leave. His work (Jeff's, not Dougie's) has appeared in Invisible City, Ocotillo Review, Kelp Journal, and elsewhere.

Final
ESCAPE

by Curtis A. Bass

Final Escape

By Curtis A. Bass

Jenna couldn't find a parking place close to the Starbuck's, so she found a spot in the grocery store lot two blocks away. Her heels clacked as she crossed the brick yard of the shopping center. She checked her watch, fearing she was late.

Good, right on time. Ryan said two o'clock.

Ryan Bronski was her lawyer. Not exactly *her* lawyer, but she felt proprietary regardless. As Assistant DA, he'd played a large role in the take down of the Randall clan, what passed for a syndicated crime family in rural North Carolina. As Dustin Randall's former girlfriend, she had been a star witness for the prosecution. No wonder the Randalls tried to kill her.

The trial had been horrific. The Randall's hired a high-priced out of state attorney to destroy Jenna's credibility. He tried to make the trial about her through character assassination. The jury decided the Randall's were guilty of so many crimes that even if Jenna were the cheap harlot the attorney painted, there was still plenty of guilt to go around.

Ryan helped her through it all, holding her hand and passing Kleenexes after each round of testimony. The Randall's tacky ploy had backfired, however. People knew the type of person Jenna was and the type of person Dustin Randall was. The Randalls had pulled every string they could to get a new venue for the trial, but the judge wouldn't allow it.

Old Man Randall received a sentence of life without parole. Dustin and his cousin, Drew, each got thirty years. The verdicts came down in March, guilty on every count, and Dustin began the first of thirty years at Odom Maximum Security Correctional Institute in rural eastern North Carolina.

The trial was over, the Randalls were in prison, spring flowers were blooming, and everything was right with the world. She hoped. Ryan hadn't told her why he wanted to see her. She feared something may have gone wrong, some wrinkle or an arcane law that would allow the Randalls to avoid prison. She prayed to God she'd never have to see Dustin Randall again.

At the coffee house door, Jenna paused to pat down her hair, seeking strands that may have escaped her ponytail. She smoothed her tweed skirt and straightened her blouse. Ryan had been so nice to her throughout the trial. She didn't want to meet him looking like a scarecrow.

Jenna pulled open the door and inhaled the deli-cious aroma of the shop. She thought coffee alone was proof there was a God. The thick, spicy scent was heavenly. She scanned the seating area but didn't notice Ryan. Then she did a double take when he waved from a nearby table. Without his lawyer costume, as she thought of it, he looked different. He had dressed comfortably in a light green polo shirt and faded jeans.

The casual dress accentuated his youthful appearance, reminding her he was only thirty years old, three years older than her. She always told him that his brown suits make him look like an old man. As Jenna approached, a grin lit up Ryan's entire face, rendering him even more handsome in her eyes. It was hard for her not to smile back and a flutter bounced around her chest.

How on earth can he still be single? Are his female work colleagues blind or something?

He stood as she reached his table.

Yes, his mama taught him some manners.

"I took the liberty of ordering you a mocha latte, extra hazelnut. I hope you don't mind," he said.

It touched Jenna that he remembered what she liked, but then they had shared a boatload of coffee over the course of the trial. The aroma evoked memo-ries of that time, some harrowing, and some intimate and sweet.

"Thanks." She considered his casual dress, wondering if it wasn't about the Randall case. But what else could it be, she wondered. We don't exactly run in the same crowds.

After brief small talk about their health and the early spring weather, Ryan got to the point.

"Jenna, I have to say that despite the unpleasantness of the trial, you have been a bright spot in my day for the past few months. I'll miss that. You've blossomed as you've gotten out from under Dustin's thumb."

He stopped and took a sip of his coffee. She wasn't sure if he expected her to say anything, but his bouncing leg let her know he was nervous. That made her nervous, but she waited to see where this was going.

"You've evolved into this wonderful, caring woman. You've become more independent, more sure of yourself and assertive. I like to think you've become the woman nature always meant you to be. And watching that unfold has had a profound effect on me. I couldn't say anything before because you were my witness and it would have been unethical, but I can't hide it any longer. I've grown fond of you and wondered if you would have dinner with me on Sunday?"

"You mean, like a date?" Jenna did not see this coming and hoped the shock didn't show on her face. He gazed at her, open and vulnerable. She had never seen him like this before. He was placing his happiness in her hands. Jenna felt a flush of heat rise in her cheeks, the surprise at his question was evident in her tone.

"Yes, like a date." He lowered his head slightly and looked at her from under his brows. She knew he used that charming look to win over female jurors. His gray eyes shone with hope.

She wasn't sure how to respond. On the one hand, he was someone she respected and looked up to; a man good and true. And he was a friend. He was also handsome and successful. What woman wouldn't want to date a man like that?

But on the other hand, would she have trouble seeing him as anything but her lawyer? They came from such different worlds. She wasn't as smart as his attorney friends and was afraid she might embarrass him. There would be complications. Besides that, she wasn't sure she wanted to date anyone after her experience with Dusty Randall.

As if reading her mind, Ryan's face fell, his confidence eroding. It dawned on her she had taken too long to answer.

He assumes I'm trying to find a way out. She gave him a reassuring smile, but he pressed on.

"I'm sorry," he said. "I've put you on the spot. I shouldn't have done that. Please forgive me."

"No, it's okay. I'm just concerned that we are from such different backgrounds."

"Yes, we are. Maybe that's part of the allure, but I want to explore this."

"Well, that's the nicest offer I've had all year. I'd love to."

* * *

Sunday evening found Ryan standing before Jenna's door, shuffling as he waited for her to answer the buzzer. Dressed in a casual shirt with a navy blazer, Jenna thought he looked good enough to eat when she spied him through the peephole.

"You look amazing," he said when she opened the door. She blushed at his compliment, looking down and nervously tucking a lock of hair behind her ear. He had seen much of her wardrobe during the trial, so Saturday evening she and Joyce had hit the mall looking for a 'date dress', as Joyce called it. His compliment assured her they had picked well. She felt chic and trendy in a bright yellow, summery dress that showed off her early tan, long legs, and dark hair.

Jenna breathed a sigh of relief when Ryan headed out of Farmington toward Greensboro. There were no really nice restaurants in their little town. Red Lobster, Chili's or, God forbid, IHOP, was the best she could hope for when she was with Dusty.

They ended up at an expensive looking steak house, with lowered lighting and quiet booths. Ryan was charming, steering clear of any talk of the trial, just exploring common interests and a little gossip.

"—So I said, 'well, it looks like you've been in my briefs'," Ryan said as the punchline to a story about a well-known humorless matron in the DA's office. Jenna covered her mouth trying not to spit out her wine in her amusement.

"I would have loved to see the look on Mavis' face," she exclaimed.

"It was priceless. But enough about me. I want to

talk about you. How are you adjusting to your new life?"

"I can't believe how much I gave up for Dusty," she said in a tremulous voice, still not used to talking about her escape from him. Her therapist told her it might take months or even years to get comfortable with discussing her past.

"Hey," Ryan whispered, reaching across the table to touch her cheek. "No tears. This is supposed to be a happy date." He frowned when she flinched away from him. "I gather you're still having the nightmares?" He pressed himself back in his chair.

She nodded, unable to speak. The horrible dreams from the memory of Dusty battering down her door in an attempt to kill her had abated, but not gone away completely. She had breathing exercises to soothe her panic attacks and prescription meds for when that wasn't enough. Sudden movements still caused her to flinch, seeking to protect herself.

"I want to kill that bastard," Ryan muttered through gritted teeth. Jenna seconded the idea.

Without Dusty's malevolent presence in her life, she had found she could flourish. She took yoga classes to find inner serenity. She returned to the ballroom and fell in love with dancing again. On a more practical note, she enrolled in a personal weapons safety class to learn to use her revolver reliably in case she had another emergency. Joyce said she had already disaster proofed her life. Her exact words were, "You've already had Dusty Randall in your life. What are the odds anything worse could happen?" *She kinda has a point.*

Ryan made her feel special. He'd ordered wine with dinner. She knew nothing about wine, but the one glass she had was delicious. She realized she was a lightweight drinker when the one glass made her feel tingly. A cheap date, as Joyce would say. She couldn't remember the last time she had such a fuss made over her. It was nice to have someone think she was worth such treatment.

Jenna feared the good-night kiss might be awkward, considering their prior lawyer-witness relationship, but when he bent his head to hers at her doorstep, she was all in. Perhaps the wine had put her in a happy place, but his kiss set off fireworks. She was definitely under his spell, drifting inside in a daze.

* * *

Ryan called her at the bank midmorning on Monday just to check in. He asked if it was okay to call her during work like this.

"Yeah, but if you do it more than once people might talk. The trial is over. You know how people are."

"Let them talk. I'm not ashamed. I hope you aren't."

"Of you? Of course not. You're totally presentable." She smirked.

"I'm glad you feel that way, because I'm aiming to

make people talk. I'd like to see you again. Friday night?"

"I have a dance lesson and then a studio function. You could come with me. Do you know any ballroom dances?"

"Let's see, I can identify my left foot and my right foot. That's about as far as I get."

"Well, if we're going to be a thing, you'll need to dance." She immediately regretted saying that, fearing she had jumped the gun. Two dates did not constitute a 'thing'.

"Oh my God, what have I gotten myself into?" he deadpanned, though she still felt the humor in his words. "Do you have time for a quick dinner between your lesson and function? You can't dance on an empty stomach."

They made plans and Friday night Jenna discovered that while Ryan's dancing skills were dreadful, he was a quick study. By the end of the night he had learned a couple of dances.

"Looks like I'm getting my dance legs," he said. "I can see why you love dancing. The people who have been doing this awhile are amazing. Then there are the people like me."

"Don't be so hard on yourself. You did great."

"You think so? Maybe I'll have to call up and ask for the 'Miss Mitzi Special'," he said, referring to the studio's beginner program.

"You start dancing and hanging around with me at dances and people will talk," Jenna teased.

And people did talk. She realized they were officially a couple when people at the office would begin a sentence with "You and Ryan..." as if they were a single person.

* * *

Being with Ryan was like a tonic for Jenna. His consideration and caring demeanor boosted her battered self-esteem more than any sessions with a therapist could. She suspected that the reason she could let her guard down just a little with Ryan was because she knew him so well. The months of late-night meetings going over testimony and trial strategy had given them a special bond.

Still, Jenna didn't want to take any chances. Her freedom was too hard won. It had taken many weeks of meetings with her therapist to find and root out the reasons for her near non-existent self-esteem. Now she worked every day to prove to herself that she was indeed a worthwhile person. She was pretty and she was fun, she told her reflection in the morning mirror. She was smart, engaging, and a generally nice human being. All the things Ryan believed and Dusty had convinced her she wasn't.

Jenna was impressed that Ryan planned dates around things she liked to do. With Dusty she had only been an accessory, arm candy when they hung out with his boorish friends. She doubted Dusty could name one thing she liked. Ryan had already sent a bouquet of her favorite flowers, lilacs, to her at work. She loved how they filled her office with a heady perfume. She also loved the envious looks from the other ladies who worked with her.

Ryan was not supportive of her marksmanship classes, however. He said that having a gun around her house just increased the chances of her shooting herself instead of an intruder. It was true that it had taken six shots to hit Dusty once at point blank range when he had broken into her apartment. But she'd had her eyes closed and her head turned. She had also been in a blind panic. Over time, she could handle the gun without being engulfed by terror. Then her aim improved.

"The classes will make sure I don't hurt myself," she'd reasoned with Ryan. "I need to be comfortable with a gun and know what I'm doing."

"You'd be safer without a gun in the house at all. The statistics are solid on that."

"Ryan, it makes me feel safe."

She knew he couldn't, or at least wouldn't, argue with that. She had explained how the aftermath of her time with Dusty was plagued by not feeling safe. Ryan had acquiesced. He even went with her to the shooting range once. Her marksmanship impressed Ryan, causing him to say, "I hope you're on my side in any future shoot out."

Jenna blushed but was so pleased. All she could think was that she had found the perfect man.

* * *

At seven pm on a Thursday in late April, there was a knock at Jenna's door. She looked through her peephole and smiled when she saw it was Ryan. The smile faded as she wondered why he was there. They didn't have a date planned and he never came over without calling first. Something must be up, and from the grim look on his face it wasn't good.

"Hey, sweetheart," he answered, giving her a quick kiss when she opened the door. He brushed past her into her living room.

"I think you should sit down," he said.

Now she knew it was bad.

"I hate to be the bearer of bad news, but you need to know. Dustin has escaped from prison."

"He what?" Jenna felt as if he had pulled a rug from under her and she was plummeting down. She was glad she was sitting.

"He was being transferred for something. I'm not clear on that yet, but a guard got too close without paying attention and Dustin grabbed his gun. He held the gun against the guard's head while he made the other guard unlock the cuffs on him and two other prisoners in the van. One of the escapees they picked up pretty quickly. He told the police that Randall shot both guards point blank and was laughing while he did it. One died. The other is in serious condition."

Jenna shook her head. "He's just gone and lost his mind. I know he was reckless and mean as a snake, but to kill someone like that, it's just crazy."

"He once tried to kill you, Jenna. He's been crazy for a long time."

126

"Yeah, but at least he thought he had a reason to kill me. Those poor guards were just doing their job."

"Well, he'll be caught, no question. And killing the guard will get him the needle. I hate it had to come at this price, but I'm not sorry he's going down. He's just a mad dog."

"So, they haven't caught him yet?"

"No. And they think he's heading this way. There's only one reason he would come here. You."

Jenna's stomach dropped even further. *Oh no. Not again.* She thought she was through with Dusty and the whole Randall clan. She wanted to be done with them permanently.

And now Dusty's coming after me.

"They should have notified both of us immediately after it happened, but someone screwed up. He escaped two days ago. He could have easily broken into your house and killed you by now. I want you to pack a bag and come with me. You can stay at my house until they catch him. I won't be able to sleep a wink if I don't know you're safe."

"I can't just move in with you, Ryan. What will people think?"

"I don't give a damn what anybody thinks. I just have to know that you're safe. I've got a security system and the police have agreed to post a uniform outside my house. Please say you'll come."

Jenna hesitated but after taking a breath she replied. "Let me get some things."

Her cell phone interrupted her thoughts when it began playing a tinny version of the song "Mamma

Mia". It was the ringtone she had assigned to her mother.

"Looks like Mama's heard," she said. "Let me get that. She's going to worry." Jenna stood and left the couch, retrieving her phone. "Hey, Mama," she said after accepting the call.

"Hey baby," said a deep rasping voice. "I've missed you."

The flash of realization buckled her knees and Jenna collapsed onto the sofa again. It was Dusty. And he had Mama's phone.

"Dusty!" was all she could say.

Ryan rushed to her side.

"Where's Mama? If you've hurt her, I swear I'll get you."

"Now don't go making promises you can't keep, sweetheart. Don't worry about your mama. She's a tough old broad. I had to knock her around a bit to get her to cooperate. You Davenports are a stubborn set of bitches."

"I'm calling the police right now," she yelled into the phone.

"Now you don't want to do that, baby. Right now your mama's doing fine. A few bruises, some blood. Maybe some broken bones, I don't know. I got excited and got into it. It's been so long since I had the chance to really work over a bitch. But if the police show up, I'll be long gone and all they'll find is your mama with a butcher knife in her heart. Or maybe I'll cut it out and take it with me."

"Dusty, don't you hurt my mama." She couldn't help crying. "Please."

"Yeah, baby, I love it when you beg. Makes me hard. Ooh yeah."

"What do you want?" she asked. "Mama ain't done nothing to you. You want something from me. What?"

"Are you forgetting that you're my girl? I heard you been whoring around with that lawyer that put me in prison. That ain't something I can let my girl get by with. People might think I'm soft. No real man lets his woman whore around without teaching her a lesson. I think it's time you and me had a talk."

She couldn't respond, but only hyperventilated into the phone.

"You come on out to your mama's house. When you get here, I'll let her go and you and me can talk about your transgressions." By 'talk' she knew he meant beat. He came close to putting her in the hospital after several of their discussions of her failings.

"Just you. Nobody else. I see anybody else but you, and that butcher knife goes right into Mama's heart."

"How do I know you ain't already killed her? Let me talk to Mama," she demanded.

"So bossy. I see I'll need to remind you how to address your lord and master. But I'm feeling generous. Hey, Mama. Say 'hey' to your girl." She could hear him move the phone away from himself. Then she heard Mama's voice.

"Don't, baby. It's a trap!"

"Shut up, bitch!" She heard a noise that sounded as if he had slapped Mama and a brief cry of pain. Jenna was a total wreck.

"It seems your mama's feeling poorly. You better get on over here and take care of her. I'd say about ten minutes. Tick tock, baby, tick tock." Then the phone went dead.

Ryan had his ear next to Jenna's and heard the entire exchange.

"You need to call the police now," he said.

"You heard what he said. He'll kill Mama!"

"And if you go there, he'll kill both of you."

"You think I don't know that? But I can't turn my back on Mama. How will I live with myself if something happens to her, and I didn't even try to help?"

"The only way you can help her is to get the police involved. They can get her out alive. If you go in there, neither of you are coming out except in body bags."

"I've got to go."

"No. I won't let you. It's suicide."

"Ryan Bronski, get the hell out of my way. You got no say over my life."

"The hell I don't. I'm in love with you. Don't you realize that? What happens to you, happens to me. I've got to have a say. Jenna, please don't do this."

Jenna leaned in and gave him a lingering kiss. "It's my mama, Ryan. I've got to."

* * *

Jenna pulled into the rutted path that led up to Mama's house, sitting back across a bean field, about a hundred yards from the state road. As her car bounced along, she noticed a blue Toyota sitting in front of the house. Probably the car Dusty stole when he escaped, she figured. She pulled up and cut the engine, mentally preparing herself for what she was about to face.

When she made the decision to come over, she knew Dusty planned to kill her and that he wouldn't let Mama go, either. He would probably kill her as well. The only thing she was uncertain about was whether he would then light out for Mexico or just kill himself.

He's always been a bit of a drama queen. The murder-suicide is so his style.

Mama's house was a turn of the century basic farmhouse. It had a wide front porch with a pair of old rocking chairs, a rusted glider and swing. She had so many fond memories of her family on this porch. *Just one more thing Dusty is trying to destroy. He ruins everything he touches,* she thought. She knocked on the door.

"It's open," Dusty's raspy voice called from inside.

She pushed the door open and walked into a large living area. At the far side Mama was sitting in a dining room chair, tied and gagged. There were black bruises forming on her face and a trickle of blood from her nose and mouth. But all in all, she seemed to be in good condition. She had a murderous look in her eyes. *Yep, Mama's all right,* she thought. *For now.*

Dusty was standing beside her mama. He had the

prison guard's weapon pointed at Mama's head. She knew he wouldn't use it yet. He wanted to make Jenna suffer longer than a quick shooting would. He was sweating profusely even though it wasn't hot inside.

His eyes were unusually wide and shifted around as if trying to find something elusive. She thought it just made him look all the crazier. His black hair was matted to his head and he'd ditched his prison clothes for an ill-fitting T-shirt and sweatpants, probably stolen from someone's clothesline.

"Come on in, sweetheart. Join the party. We've been waiting for you."

"Let Mama go, Dusty. You said if I came, you'd let her go. Here I am."

"Yeah, funny thing about that. I can't believe you actually fell for it. I don't remember you being that stupid." He laughed as if it were funny.

"You bastard."

"Hey, you don't talk about your fiancé like that," he said in a warning tone.

"You're not my fiancé, Dustin Randall. You're just a low life punk, a bully, a redneck son of a bitch." It felt so good to get it out, to actually say the words she'd been longing to say for so long. His face reddened. "Yeah, the truth hurts, don't it."

"Raise your hands. I want to make sure you ain't got anything." She did as he told her.

"Now pull out your pockets. You might have a knife or something in there." Again, she complied.

"Good. Now get over here," he pointed to a chair near Mama's. There was rope and duct tape on the floor beside it. "I'm gonna get you good and secured and then we can work on your manners." His evil grin had returned.

She realized the setup was the best she could hope for to use her plan. Dusty was clear of Mama, focusing on Jenna. Acting frightened she gave him a wide berth, moving to the right, approaching the chair.

This allowed her to keep her left side to him. He couldn't see her right hand as it crept to the back of her waist. He didn't notice when she slipped the revolver out of her waistband.

Jenna stopped ten feet from the chair. *Time to get his gun off Mama.*

"Go on. Get in the chair," Dusty said.

"No."

"You heard me, bitch. Do as I say."

"I said no. I'm not playing your sick game. You're just a yellow-bellied coward who gets off on hurting people who are weaker than you. You don't have the balls to take on a real man. You're just a pansy loser. I bet you're somebody's bitch in prison." She laid it on thick. She wanted to get him really mad. "You take it up the ass, don't you?"

"You don't want to test me, girl. Now move!" Dusty roared, getting redder in the face.

"Nope. Ain't doing it. So who's your prison boyfriend?"

"I said git!" Dusty swiveled the gun from Mama's head to point at Jenna. *Ok, good. He's not pointing it at Mama. Now to get him to lower the gun.*

"Fuck you. Make me," she taunted.

Dusty's eyes grew even wider as what composure he had snapped. He charged Jenna, lowering the gun as he moved. Jenna had just enough time to pull her revolver from behind her, take a quick aim at his groin and fire. The deafening blast made Mama squeak. Dusty went down fast. He quickly rolled into a fetal position, grabbing his crotch, and screaming.

Jenna kicked the gun Dusty had been holding across the floor. Then she kicked Dusty, just because she could. Ryan burst through the door, gun in one hand and cell phone in the other. He had been waiting in the backseat of her car. He said he had already contacted the 911 operator and help was on the way. Grabbing Jenna, he held her tightly, as if he never wanted to let go. Then they untied Mama. Thankfully, her wounds were only superficial.

When the first EMTs came rushing in, she directed them away from Dusty and toward Mama. Luckily for him there were two technicians, so they split up. Poor Dusty was still screaming and bleeding profusely. The EMT had a devil of a time getting him out of the fetal position to strap him on a gurney.

By the time they had him packed up, the place was swarming with police. That was when all her steel shattered, and Jenna became a basket case. But Ryan was there to take care of her.

* * *

A few days later Ryan gave her the official word on Dusty.

"He will be tried for the murder of a prison police officer, among other things. The state is asking for the death penalty."

"Good. I hope they get it," she said. "Then he can sit alone in his cell for the next fifteen years, no one to visit him but his mama, and I hear she may be under indictment. They say that many death row inmates eventually go crazy from the boredom with no human contact and nothing to do but jerk off."

"Well, ah, he won't be doing that anymore either. Your shot actually severed his penis and shattered his balls. Makes me hurt to think about it. He's going to need a catheter to piss and there's no chance of him diluting the quality of the gene pool ever again."

Jenna considered her choice of where to shoot Dusty. Maybe what she did was over the top, but she wanted to hurt him. She wanted to hurt him bad, but not kill him. *Let the state do that.* He lived on his machismo so taking that away seemed appropriate.

But it was time to forget Dustin Randall and look to her own life again.

"So, Ryan. About that sleepover you mentioned. Is that offer still on the table?"

* * *

Curtis A. Bass (CurtisStories.blog) from the American south, writes short stories in a variety of genres including science fiction, horror, mystery, and young adult. He's had stories published in online and print journals such as Youth Imagination, Fabula Argentea, Page & Spine, and the anthologies 2020 in a Flash, Best of 2020; The Protest Diaries; Worlds Within; and Screaming in the Night. Water Dragon Press recently published his stand-alone novelette. When not writing, he prefers to stay active ballroom dancing or downhill skiing. He is currently working on his second novel while his first remains hidden in a drawer.

We Make Noise in
Quiet Places

by Christian Flynn

We Make Noise in Quiet Places

By Christian Flynn

When I first met Sandy Aberdeen, I was 16 and didn't think much of her. I saw her band a few times at a bowling alley and they played good, if derivative, post-punk. I remember little other than teenage awkwardness and weed. She was older— mid twenties, and always had young cool people in her orbit. I talked to her after and she said she was going off to New York on a record deal or something, and I said I was going off to college. I forgot the name of the band soon after and that was all.

I went to Emerson for film but it didn't suit me. I moped around with my boyfriend for two years, never made friends, came out as a lesbian, broke up with my boyfriend, got sick, and went back to my boring hometown.

In my Mom's basement, I could not get out of bed

without help. I fought it by watching movies. I shaved my head: not as an act of defiance and self discovery but as surrender, a joyful act of giving up. I ate slowly. I messaged strangers online.

One day, when I'd regained the strength to walk, I went downtown to the local grocery store to get myself some ingredients for a soup I wanted to cook with my Mom. I looked across the street and right in a spot I'd seen a million times in my childhood was a cool, hip, young coffeeshop, the type my town would never tolerate. I walked in and there was Sandy, holding court on a leather couch to a group of folks with piercings and tattoos and weird haircuts.

"Sandy," I said.

Everyone turned towards me. I got a good look at Sandy. She must've been in her mid thirties. She hadn't lost any of her piercings. The haircut was even better. She had even more tats.

She said my name and made a little gesture. I walked over and sat down beside her on the leather couch.

"What the fuck you been up to soldier?" She said.

"Oh you know," I said. "Losing and finding myself."

Everyone laughed. I don't know where that charisma came from.

"What's with that haircut? Gender thing?"

"Yeah a couple of people have called me that."

Again they laughed. Again, charisma.

"We're about to go to a rock show tonight," Sandy said. "Do you wanna come?"

"Do I have a choice?"

They laughed.

"Nah."

We piled into a filthy little five-seater with "I Love You Butch" in faded spray paint on the front. I thought back to teenage parties, movie nights. On the way I asked Sandy if she was visiting from the city and she told me she lived here. I asked her wasn't New York better and she waved me off.

"When you're in a city like that," she said, "and your whole thing is queer and your friends and network and stuff. . . there's no danger, there's no fun. But when you're around a place like this you know, you can ruffle some feathers. You can save a kids life, you know? You can open a *coffeeshop*."

I got back from the rock show at 3 am. I snuck through the back door so I wouldn't wake my Mom up. I was a teenager, but sick this time. I lay in my childhood bed, staring up at the ceiling and felt my body ache, my stomach lurch into nausea.

At the show, Sandy got drunk and it made her incompetent and flirty. The friends in the car fanned out into friends at the rock show and I was overwhelmed at the people but I felt more like myself than I had in millennia. I danced—I'd forgotten I liked to dance. I was on the verge of forming a thought about this when I woke up.

* * *

Two weeks later I ran into Sandy again. I had gone to get a burrito from a new place that opened and I was eating it on the street when I looked up and saw some punks standing outside a record shop. I crossed the street and walked past the punk and inside there were posters of bands and gore and porn and some more punks.

I asked the pierced-up girl behind the counter how the hell a shop like this survived in this town. She snort-laughed. I saw a flier on the counter for a poetry reading Friday that Sandy was putting together at a bar in town I'd never heard of.

Friday came and I wore my Slits shirt and my old ripped jean jacket but that's about all the strength I could muster up. I walked down from my house and the bar was a little over a mile but the air was clean and cold and I put on Lou Reed for the first time in a long time.

I walked into the bar and the guy checked my ID and I gave it to him and it was all brown with the wood and graffiti all over the walls. I stood close to the back and the place filled up and people got drinks and some sat down and others stood to watch.

Sandy got up and started to perform and I looked out over the crowd. Only like 20 people but they all looked excited for her and I knew no one. I looked at the bartender with the tattoos and the Japanese Taxi Driver poster hanging above. The seedy lights, the rubber smell, the TV screen with Return of the Living Dead playing on mute.

I closed my eyes.

At 2 AM I had Sandy's tongue down my throat against the bar. She asked if I wanted her to take me home with her and I said yes but I didn't really care that much.

* * *

Three months later I ran into Sandy again. Fall turned to winter and my buddy Jada was back from Cornell on winter break. We were in the diner and it was dark at 5 O'clock. I had a Ruben and she had eggs and she was telling me about her semester when I caught Sandy out of the corner of my eye and stared. She was with a guy with patches on his jacket and they were talking and laughing a lot.

"Who's that?" Jada said.

"A woman I went home with a few months back."

"A woman you went *home with?*"

"Yeah."

"In this town?"

"I guess."

"Huh."

After dinner we drove out towards the neighboring town and parked down by their waterfront and walked around and talked. After a half hour Jada's knees started to hurt but I was feeling good out in the cold so I kept walking and she went back to the car.

I walked out towards the river even though the breeze off it was freezing. I pulled my hood up against the cold and knelt down and picked up a smooth rock. Before I could skip it I heard sniffling and turned and a woman was walking alone.

"Sandy."

She looked up at me like she wasn't surprised. Her eyes were red and puffy and her makeup was messed up. She looked at me for a while. Her eyes and cheeks did that scrunched up thing that makes you look like a kid before you start crying.

"Oh, hey soldier."

We stood there with our hands in our pockets, vaguely crying, about 6 feet of distance, staring at each other, shoulders up to brace against the cold.

I didn't say anything. Anything I could've said would've been dumb.

* * *

Three months later Sandy finally asked me out. I was lying in bed, sort of unable to walk, when I got the call.

"You wanna get, like, a drink or something?"

"Yeah."

"Alright, I'll meet you at the place I did the reading. At like. . ."

"Yeah."

It was rainy and cold out. It was springtime. I dug out my sweater with a skull on it and for the first time pulled the tape I'd bought like a few months earlier out of the drawer and taped my tits down.

I put on the tight black jeans I wore every day and added some black boots to it to make them look nice. I put my blue raincoat on. In the mirror I was too skinny and my eyes looked hollowed out but I liked how I looked a lot.

I walked down to the bar but I had to stop a few times to sit down. I'd find a curb and let my ass get wet and put on "Deathconsciousness" and temporarily drown.

I got to the bar and Sandy was spotless and dry and had a streak of pink in her hair and a military jacket with a patch on the back for a metal band I never heard of. She was over in the corner with a beer in front of her and he was pulled into herself. I walked over and sat beside her.

"Dude you're drenched."

"Yeah."

"Why didn't you tell me, I could've picked you up."

"Oh. I didn't know. . ."

"Yeah. . ."

My body ached and I thought I might fall over but she bought me a drink and I was happy to be there, happy to be out. We chatted about the band on her back a bit and I told her about a few metal bands I knew back in Boston and she said she'd check them out.

She asked me about The Slits 'cause she remembered I had worn their shirt and I told her about all the history and how much I loved Ari Up.

"Hey Sandy."

"Yeah."

"You had a band right? Whatever happened to that?"

She looked away from me.

"Ah you know, bands are a lot of drama," She said.

"Yeah but didn't you guys have a record deal?"

"Yeah."

"And you guys were good man I remember seeing you in high school and stuff."

She looked back at me with something behind her eyes.

"Sometimes, Soldier, it's easier to wonder 'what if' than watch it all come crashing down."

"Yeah but—"

"What about you, why did you drop out of film college?"

I didn't answer. It seemed too obvious.

After that we got back to talking about metal and she drove us back to the place she was renting and we smoked cigarettes on the lawn.

"Something nice about being in the suburbs is you have some space, you know?" She said. "You can do your little office job and make an impact on your time off when you know your time off. Everyone's not always on."

"You have an office job?"

"Hey, don't look at me like that man. I can buy us drinks. Help my friends out. I helped Mar save up the money to open that coffeeshop. My friend's running that record store. You know? Nothing punk rock about shooting up and starving. I try to help out."

I felt nauseous and I leaned over against her house. Sandy came over and asked me if she could help and I don't normally but I let her hold my arm and take me into the house. She lay me down on the couch and held me.

"I hate cancer," was all I could say. "I hate cancer so much."

* * *

Around 4 am I woke up to go to the bathroom and the name of Sandy's band finally came to me. I looked them up, they were more popular than I realized.

Right below their Wikipedia page I saw a reddit thread titled "The Truth About Sandy Aberdeen" and a link to a Google Doc.

I clicked my phone black and put it back in my pocket. I went to the couch and lay back down in her arms.

* * *

Christian Flynn (they) is a writer based in Ridgewood, Queens. Their full length plays include Everyone in New York is Beautiful (2024 O'Neill NPC Semi-Finalist, Cypress Productions), and Gamepiece (The Center at West Park, Purgatory). Their writing has been published by Horror Press, Cusper Magazine, and 13tracks.

To Die Unseen

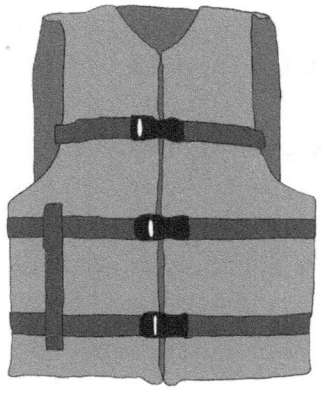

by Warren Benedetto

To Die Unseen

By Warren Benedetto

Every few years, you'll hear a miraculous story about survival at sea, about some wayward fisherman found adrift in on a piece of wreckage thousands of miles from the nearest shore. You'll hear about his rescue by a passing cargo ship that just happened to spot him on its radar, about how he survived on a diet of raw fish, fresh piss, and the occasional seagull he managed to strangle with his bare hands.

You'll see the shaky post-rescue smartphone video of him with a blanket draped over his shoulders as he sips hot tea from a dented metal cup. You'll marvel at the man's strength of character. His will to survive. His unshakable faith in God.

This is not one of those stories.

Because, first of all, fuck God. I don't want a miraculous rescue. I want a miraculous not-getting-lost-at-sea-in-the-first-place. I want a God that says, "You know, maybe I *won't* send a rogue wave to obliterate Henry's sailboat while he sleeps."

A God that doesn't stand idly by while I desperately try to save myself from the sinking wreckage. Hell, I'd settle for a God that shatters my skull on the bulkhead, so at least I'd be unconscious while I drown.

Instead, I'm sitting on a fiberglass box that bobbed to the surface a few feet from where my wife went under for the last time. The box is long and narrow, delightfully coffin-sized, with just enough space for me to lay flat without my limbs dangling over the edge. And you know what's inside? Lifejackets. Fucking *lifejackets*. Isn't that a hoot? Isn't that just the height of comedy? At least God has a sense of humor.

What's even funnier is that the box is upside down, so the lid is underwater, making the lifejackets inside maddeningly out of reach. I could theoretically slip into the water and flip the box over so I could open the lid, but fuck that. I'm not getting in the water again. Not after what happened to Annie. Not with that eye down there, looking at me. Staring at me. *Watching* me.

I have no sense of perspective, so I can't tell how big the eye is. But from where I sit, it looks like it's the size of a dinner table, with a pale blue iris that shimmers in the sunlight and glows in the light of the moon. It's sunken in a socket of glistening black flesh under an eyelid that occasionally closes in a slow, languid blink.

I can't discern any other features, so I don't know what kind of face it belongs to. Is it a whale? At first, I figured it must be. Then I realized that whales need to breathe, and whatever the thing with the eye is, it hasn't surfaced for air in the three days I've been floating out here.

If it's not a whale, then what is it? A giant squid? A fucking Kraken? What else is big enough to have an eye that huge? And whatever it is, why does it keep ogling me? If it wanted to kill me, it certainly could have done it by now. All it needs to do is knock me into the water and then suck me into its mouth like a piece of krill. I'd go down whole—it wouldn't even need to chew. But instead, it's gaping at me like I'm its pet goldfish. Shit, maybe I am. Maybe it wasn't a rogue wave that hit us. Maybe our boat got snatched up and dropped into some kind of giant cosmic fishbowl. Then God gave it a good shake, and now he's waiting to see what I'll do next.

I'll tell you what I'd *like* to do. I'd like to drive a spear into that eye, to puncture that endlessly staring orb. I want to feel it pop, to watch it fill with a stinging mix of blood and seawater. That'll teach it.

I'm not its fucking pet. I'm not here for its entertainment. I'm a human being. I have a name. I have parents. I have people who love me, people who are probably looking for me right now. Why haven't they found me? Where's the Coast Guard? Where are the search helicopters? Where's *my* passing cargo ship?

It's the eye of God. It must be. He's watching me. He sees me. And he knows. He knows what's in my heart. He knows the lie that I've been living. He knows my reconciliation with Annie was a farce, a ploy to get her to join me on the boat for the weekend. He knows only one of us was supposed to return home. He knows my cover story, the carefully constructed lie I intended to tell the police. He knows I could have saved her when she begged for help. He knows that even as I fought for my own survival, a part of me was grateful that I didn't have to drown her myself.

And yet, what's he doing about it? Nothing. Just sitting back and enjoying the view. Typical God shit. He could help me if he wanted. Or he could kill me, quick and easy. I'd respect that—I deserve it. At least that would show some balls.

But what I can't respect is a God that just watches. A docile God. An impotent God. A limp-dick God who's afraid to take matters into his own hands. I'm not like him. I take action. When Annie filed for divorce, I didn't just sit by and let it happen. I made a plan and executed it, one way or another. And that's what I'm going to do again. Because you know what else is in this box I'm sitting on, besides lifejackets?

My spear gun.

I'm tired of being watched. The time has come for me to darken that stare. If I'm to die out here, I'll die unseen.

Better a blind God than a passive one.

* * *

Warren Benedetto writes dark fiction about horrible people, horrible places, and horrible things. He is an award-winning author who has published over 260 stories, appearing in publications such as Dark Matter Magazine, Fantasy Magazine, and The Dread Machine; on podcasts such as The NoSleep Podcast, Tales to Terrify, and Chilling Tales For Dark Nights; and in anthologies from Apex Magazine, Tenebrous Press, Scare Street, and many more. He also works in the video game industry, where he holds 50+ patents for various types of gaming technology. For more information, visit warrenbenedetto.com and follow @warrenbenedetto on Twitter and Instagram.

REAPERS.

by Noah Browning

Reapers

By Noah Browning

Ever had your mind screwed with? It's not a good feeling. To be honest, I'm still trying to grasp what exactly I lost.

I was knocked out. It felt like I was suspended in the air as I floated in thick darkness. Fire would touch my body at moments for a time, but it stayed in my mind. It felt full for a moment, but everything was being burnt away. Now, it was just full of smoke just trying to make mannequins of people that were probably there before.

My eyes shot open, lights passing me as I floated across the floor. I leaned to my left and saw a hand-cuff keeping me attached to a gurney. Concepts came to me naturally like what a light was, and what I was laying on, but personal stuff was nothing but blanks.

I should've panicked right there, but I think I was

still high on some kind of pills they had me on. Something about the way the lights looked to me was evident enough that whatever I was on was wearing off.

We came to a stop and the gurney tilted forward. I fell face-first onto a padded floor, and the metal door slammed shut behind me.

I tried to push myself back up, but my arms gave out. My body was still shaking from whatever happened.

That's the worst part. I knew something had happened, what exactly was void. If it weren't for the drugs, I probably would've broken down.

I heard footsteps outside the room. I tried to move, but all I did was flop over onto my back.

The door opened slowly. In the doorway stood a man with pale skin. He wore a black business suit, a purple shirt, and a white tie.

"Well," he said. "They came out good didn't they?"

He leaned down to get a better look at me. He lifted a pair of sunglasses with red rounded lenses off. He had distinct Asian facial features, but from where specifically I couldn't tell. He tossed a tablet down next to me.

"When the pills wear off, use that to buy yourself some clothes," he said.

After what felt like an eternity, I was able to move around. I glanced at the tablet, before dragging my finger against the ends of the padded walls. I couldn't gather any sort of breaks in the seams or any openings to abuse. I understood it was either get some clothes and do whatever that guy wanted, or rot in here forever.

I picked up the tablet and turned it on. It started on a white screen with two blue circles chasing each other. Words that read "Please wait as we scan your face" spun around and hopped every few seconds. After a few moments, the circles disappeared and new words that read "Welcome Subject 88" appeared. The screen faded to white and a new screen appeared full of clothing items.

There were menus upon menus. Shirts, jackets, pants, and shoes, as well as a section titled: New items. I tapped the new items section and saw a leather jacket that caught my eye. It was a nice electric purple leather jacket with studs near the wrist lining. It also had this nice big patch on the back that read "Nuke L.A." I had no idea what L.A. was at the time, but I thought it sounded badass.

After that, my clothing choices slipped into place. Torn black jeans, a white tank top, and black Timberland boots. It all added up. I put it all together and pressed the make order button. The screen turned white again and text appeared that read "Please wait as your order is sent to you. Please keep this tablet with you after your order has arrived."

I sat in the room until a box fell from the roof. I looked up for a moment to see where it came from, but I only saw some kind of panel slip into place too quickly for anyone to react to. I opened the box and saw that everything I ordered was there.

I slipped everything on. It fit perfectly.

The tablet chimed with a bell sound and a bit-crushed voice said "Thank you!" from the speaker.

The door to the room opened up once more. The same man from earlier was standing in the doorway.

"Finally dressed?" he said. "That's good. Follow me to my office, would you?"

I thought about using the tablet to bash his head in right there, maybe finding a way out of wherever I was, but something told me that wouldn't end well for me. Instead, I followed him like a dog and held the tablet close to me.

Once outside the room, I saw that I was in a void of a hallway. It was hauntingly white with fluorescent lights lining the roof.

The man walked down the hallway.

"How's your brain feeling?" he asked. "Nothing burning? No intense pressure in the back of your head?"

I remained silent.

"If you do feel any of that, you should let someone know, wouldn't want you having a stroke now, right?"

We continued in silence.

"Y'know," he said. "Normally people are more talkative after I let them out."

I remained silent. He turned around to look at me.

"Strong silent type, huh? They're gonna *love* you."

He grabbed a brass doorknob and opened an office. It was a large office covered in cold steel. The only thing of any color was the tank of koi fish behind the desk. The man sat down behind the desk and gestured to me to sit down in front of him.

"Welcome to the program. You can call me Mashima. Nice to meet you."

I tested him with my eyes. Something about the casual way he presented himself was off to me. It was disingenuous like he was trying to lull me into a state of comfort. I wasn't willing to let that happen.

"So, look, as of today you'll be referred to as Ghost," he said.

"That's my name?" I replied.

"Oh, so now you talk? I thought for a moment you were deaf or something."

He took out a manilla folder from his desk drawer and placed it on the desktop.

"Here's all the paperwork to give if a cop asks you anything."

I opened the manilla folder. There were only two pieces of paper with photo paper clipped onto them. The photo was of a man with dark skin, closely shaved hair, and stubble. I assumed that was me, I was right. I read everything but one thing caught my eye. It read: Job Position: Reaper.

"What's a Reaper?" I asked.

"You'll put it together as you go," Mashima replied.

"What if I don't want to be a *Reaper*?"

Mashima leaned forward and made direct eye contact with me. "Who and what you are is whatever the hell I say you are."

I raised my eyebrow at him.

He pointed at the tablet I had in my other hand. "You should pick your weapons of choice."

I lifted the tablet to my face. There was a new list

of weapons, but one that caught my eye was a chrome bat. I placed the tablet on the table. He gave me a confused look.

"A bat? You don't want anything else? No gun? Is that the idea? To kill yourself."

"I like the bat."

"Alright, you can grab whatever you need later anyway. Now, let's get you out of my office."

I was escorted by a couple of women wearing yellow uniforms into a break room of sorts. When we got to the door, one of the women looked at me and said "You're being paired up with Tab, if she gives you an order. You listen. Do you understand?"

I gave her a look and walked through the door.

Inside the break room were a couple of round tables, a couch, and some kind of punk song playing from somewhere. The news was playing on a screen in the wall, but the music was swallowing up whatever it could have been saying.

There were a few other people in the room. A guy wearing a red bathrobe was sitting on the couch. He swiveled his head around towards me and rotated a bottle of beer around in his hand.

"Welcome!" he said. "Wel. . . Welcome to the place."

I stood silent for a few moments trying to get a read for the room.

"Anyone in here named Tab?" I asked.

A refrigerator door was slammed shut. The closing of that door revealed a girl with green hair. She gave me an irritated look.

"Name's Tab," she said. "Who's asking?"

"I'm supposed to work with you," I replied.

"Oh. Look at this guy, we got a freshie in here."

I heard the sound of a toilet being flushed. A man wearing sunglasses with navy blue lenses walked out of the bathroom.

"A freshie, huh?" the man said. "He's got some style on him."

"He's working with me," said Tab.

"Well maybe. . . could you get him to get me a chick off. . . the street?" said the man in the bathrobe. After that, he hiccuped, laughed, and took a large swig of his beer.

"The drunk on the couch is Bone. We think he used to be a Wino before he got scooped," said Tab. "The guy who wears sunglasses indoors is Shades."

Tab opened up one of the cabinets and pulled out a bag of chips. She held them out to me.

"You hungry?" she asked.

I shook my head no.

"Alright, but you should eat. The pills they put you on mess you up if you don't."

I held my hand out.

She placed the chips in my hand, I threw some potato chips in my mouth. Getting a closer look at Tab, she was a surprisingly tall woman, or maybe I'm just short. She stood up to my eye level, and she had dark tanned skin. I could make out something of a tattoo running down her neck, but it was cut off by her shirt line.

"If you're working with Tab. . . she'll kill ya. . ." said Bone. "She's the oldest. . . one here."

"Shut up, Bone," said Tab. "You worked with me and you're still alive."

"Oh yeah? And I'm the spitting image of healthy!"

They both laughed at his one-liner. I just stood silent.

"Well c'mon tall, dark, and dangerous," said Bone. "The hell is your name?"

I didn't respond.

"You gonna keep being an ass, or talk like a big boy?"

"They said my name was Ghost."

"Ghost, huh? What a weird name."

"You all have weird names."

"Bone is a cool name."

"Sure."

A small chirping song played from around Tab's area. She held out her forearm and looked at the backside of it. The backside of her arm was projecting text. It was like when you place a flashlight behind a blanket, except the blanket was her skin and the light was text.

"That's quicker than usual," she said. "C'mon, Ghost, your first job is already here."

"Go get 'em Casper!" said Bone.

Tab and I walked through this concrete parking garage. She pulled out some car keys and clicked a button, which was followed by *BLIP BLIP* coming out of an older, red car. She opened the trunk, took a black duffle bag out, and tossed it into the backseat.

It clunked into the backseat with the sound of plastic and metal crashing into each other.

"What's in the bag?" I asked.

"Guns," she replied. "A lot of guns."

I shrugged in response and went to sit in the passenger seat. I heard footsteps rapidly approaching us with some heavy breathing.

"Wait! Wait!" shouted a voice.

I turned to look and noticed it was Shades holding a gray, cardboard box. He stopped in front of me and held out the box.

"Your stuff came a little late," he said. "It'd be bad for you if you didn't get this before going out. Wouldn't want assets like us getting hurt, right?"

"Uh. . . right," I responded. "Thanks."

I took the box and sat in the passenger's seat.

"Ready now?" asked Tab.

I nodded.

* * *

I rode inside Tab's old car. For some reason, I thought the outside city would be mostly neon, but most buildings had a large screen with some kind of shifting advertisements on it. I would've marveled at all the colors that were flooding my senses if they weren't trying to sell me something every ten seconds.

We were stuck in traffic, but Tab didn't seem to mind. She was playing a rap song on the radio.

"Hey, hey, hey," she caught my attention. "Listen to this part."

She turned the knob on the radio and the song became louder.

"Past, present, ripped and now defenseless/ Now all I can do is fence sit/ Memory can be reconstructionist/ Understand the function of it, yeah," she rapped along to the song. "That's hard as hell, right?"

I shrugged.

"Damn, you're no fun, you know that, Ghost? Just say something, it's not like we've got anything to do."

I looked out the window to see an ad for something called a smart bullet.

"What do you think your job was before you got scooped?" she asked.

"I don't know," I replied.

"Well, I think I was an Orthodontist."

"Is this a religion or something?" I smirked.

"Damn, they must've scooped too much from you," she chuckled. "Looks like you have a soul after all. I was scared you were a bot or some crap like that."

I looked over at her. "Why do you think you were an Orthodontist?"

"Look at how shiny my teeth are," she gave me a huge smile. "You think any other job would have teeth that clean?"

"An actress?"

"Nah. I can't see myself as an actress. I'd overdose on something."

"That's depressing."

"That's reality sometimes, Ghosty. It's not like we can ignore it."

There was an awkward silence.

"Y'know what I think you were, Ghosty?" she asked.

"What?" I replied.

"I think you were a punk. You just seem like the type to do shady jobs. I mean, only a punk would be dressed like you."

I raised my left eyebrow. "Oh yeah? Maybe that's a good thing."

"What makes you say that?"

"Cause I'll carry your ass on this job."

"Pfft. Yeah right."

There was another moment of silence.

"Y'know what, Ghosty?" she said. "You're alright."

"Thanks?" I said. "Hey, can I ask you something?"

"Sure."

"The hell does Tab mean?"

"It's short for Tabula Rasa."

"Huh?"

"It means having a clean mind or something like that. It's an old phrase. They thought they were real funny when they named me that. Smug ass Mashima was trying not to laugh when he did it."

"I guess I'm not the only one who hates that guy."

"You're not. The only one who likes that corporate jackass is Shades. Hell, I wouldn't be surprised if he sucked his-"

Her arm interrupted what she was going to say by

chirping and saying "The target location has changed. The target is now in the Historic District."

"Oh come on!" she cried. "Well, now we're gonna have to turn around at some point. Be ready for this to get messy, Ghost."

* * *

We took far longer than we probably should have to get to the target. Tab looked pissed the whole time, I think she was chewing her tongue to ease her tension. We eventually parked by a strip club. Tab looked at her arm and checked the target information. A face appeared. The face was of a guy with tattoos all over his face, and he had pinkish skin. It could have been from sunburn or modded skin pigment. The point was, he was easy to identify.

"For a mod thief," said Tab. "He doesn't try to hide, huh?"

"Guess not," I replied.

I looked out the windshield and noticed the pink-skinned guy strut out of the strip club with a girl around his arm. I slapped Tab's arm to grab her attention.

"OW!" she yelled. "You short-circuiting, Ghost?"

I replied by pointing at our target.

"Alright! Let's sit back for a minute, and make sure he isn't modded more than he should be."

Tab stretched and grabbed the bag in the back-seat. She dug through and pulled out a weird, chrome ball. She placed it on the dashboard and a lens grew out of its side. She turned the ball so that the lens was facing the target. It took a couple of moments before it blipped. Tab took the ball and looked at its top. Words formed across its surface. The words read: Mods: 1 Illegally Obtained EMP hidden in the left arm.

"EMP?!" shouted Tab.

She leaned back in her seat for a moment and looked at the ceiling of the car. She chuckled and looked over at me. Her face became aggressive and she yanked me forward by my jacket collar.

"Ghost? Are you a snitch?" she asked.

"What?" I sputtered.

"Ghost. I've got an idea, but if you snitch, I swear to whatever God that may exist I'll put your head to the curb!"

"Alright! I won't say anything."

"Don't say a damn thing!"

"I won't!"

"Good!"

I turned my head and saw the target looking directly at us through the windshield.

"Tab?" I said.

She craned her head and saw the target. She rolled her window down and stuck her head out.

"What's good?" she asked.

"I'm. . . alright. . ." replied the pink man.

Tab exited the car. "You're Pinky, right?"

"Yeah, that's me. Who's asking?"

"I've got a new mod for you."

"Huh? I thought Marco was coming to deliver."

"He was, but he woke up with an STI."

"Oh damn, for real?"

"Yeah, man."

"So. . . what do I call you?"

"Me? I'm Twitch. Look, I got somewhere else to be soon. Just follow me to the trunk, alright? The mod should be in there."

"Alright," Pinky looked at me through the windshield. "Who's the punk in the car?"

"Don't worry about him. That's Nukey. He's got to get to the airport in a bit, that's why we gotta make this deal ASAP."

Tab and Pinky walked to the back of the car. I had no idea what she was even doing. I was trying not to die of anxiety.

Tab opened the trunk. Pinky looked confused.

"Where's the. . . mod?" asked Pinky.

Tab grabbed Pinky by the throat with her left arm. Her arm's flesh spread out for a moment to reveal mechanical elements. Her arm made a *KSSH* sound, and Pinky fell unconscious. Tab tossed him into the trunk and slammed it shut. She walked toward the driver's seat and entered the car.

I looked at her with a bewildered look.

"He's fine," she said. "My left arm has a knockout mod. He'll be out probably all day."

"Okay. . . but why is he. . . in the trunk?"

"You really wanna be stopped by cops every ten seconds?"

"No."

"Then keep your cool. We've got someone to meet with."

We stood in front of a door lined with red Christmas lights in an alleyway. I had Pinky's unconscious body leaning up against me.

"So, what's this place?" I asked.

"Guy's a modder," said Tab. "Just... don't ask too many questions. He can be. . . jumpy."

Tab knocked on the door. A voice echoed from behind the door.

"JESUS CHRIST!" the voice yelled. "They always knock at the worst time! What do you want?"

"It's me," said Tab.

"Who's me?"

Tab sighed in annoyance. "Tab."

"Oh hey, Tab! Why're you here? I was. . . in the middle of something."

"I've got a rare mod. I wanted you to look at it."

"Give me a minute."

We could hear some doors opening, something clanking, and doors being shut. The door unlocked, and the person behind it opened it. He was a short man with tanned skin, kind of copper-like in its tone.

"I wasn't working on a robotic romantic partner," he said.

I was confused.

"Say I wasn't working on it," he said.

"Uh. . . I wasn't—" I said.

"NO! Are you deaf or brain-dead? *SAY* that *I* was not working on a robotic romantic partner."

"You. . . weren't working on a robotic romantic partner?"

"Was that a question?"

"No."

"Alright, fair enough. I'm Jiiga."

He held out his hand for a handshake. He noticed the guy I was carrying and rescinded his offer.

"Oh right," said Jiiga. "This the guy with the mod? Why is he out cold?"

"Working hazard," said Tab.

"Works for me, let's get to work."

* * *

Jiiga viciously typed away at his keyboard as Pinky was laid on a makeshift surgical bed. He had an IV stabbed into the inside of his elbow. Surgical tools sat on a metal tray sitting atop a set of metal legs.

"Pretty rare mod this guy has," said Jiiga. "It's got no ID chip in it, so it's probably illegally obtained."

"Yeah, we know that," said Tab.

"What do you want me to do? Just take it out of him?"

"Could you. . . install it into someone else?"

"Well. . ." he stared at Tab for a moment. "It's a mod for an arm, you already got a mod in each arm. However. . ."

Jiiga pounced next to me and yanked my right arm. He traced my veins with his free hand, then repeated the same process for my left arm.

"This guy is mod free," said Jiiga. "Also, he's got beautiful veins, might I add."

"Mod him," said Tab.

"What?" I said. "You're not even going to ask if I want to be modded?"

Tab looked at me. "Do you want to be modded?"

"I don't even know why I would be modded."

Tab leaned in closer to me. She set her lips an inch away from my ear.

"We're gonna get out of this Reaper business," she whispered. "That mod is our ticket out. If we EMP the place, all the tech will go down and we'll be free."

She pulled away from me. I looked at her, and then at Jiiga.

"Mod me."

* * *

I woke up to my head hitting the passenger seat window in Tab's car. We were back outside and driving through the street. Gigantic screens upon gigantic screens light up the night with hyper-consumerist glory.

The synthetic skin was itchy as hell over my mod. I couldn't help but scratch at it when I could.

"Stop scratching it," said Tab. "You'll screw up the skin that way."

"Sorry," I replied.

I looked around the car to see Pinky wasn't with us anymore.

"What happened?" I asked.

"Well, the anesthetics knocked you out longer than we anticipated. The surgery went well though."

"Where is. . . Pinky?"

"Oh, Jiiga and I dumped him off in a dumpster a mile away from his spot. We implanted a memory in his head that he was jumped by a Pimp he forgot to pay off and was left in a dumpster. Leaves no trail for him to track us through."

"You wiped his memory?"

"What? No! Were you listening? We planted a fake memory. He's still who he is, just with a slightly different way to remember what happened a few hours ago."

"Is that what they did to us?"

"No. . . I. . . I don't know. We really shouldn't think about that, okay?"

I leaned back in my seat and kept quiet. The ride was silent for at least half an hour. I stared at every ad we passed by. Many were trying to sell people guns, or eating foods that only the Corporations provided. One ad made the argument that processed food allowed you to live longer in comparison to eating naturally grown food.

All the colors were like a trap made by a predator. A predator that learned how to farm, the only problem was that it had been using all of us as livestock. It was beautiful on the surface, but all I could think was I hated this city.

I had no clue what the place was even called. It could have been whatever L.A. was, but I knew it wasn't where people belonged to be.

I leaned over to Tab.

"Where are you going after we get out?" I asked.

"Anywhere but here," she said. "I've heard there's

a place in space you can live in. I've never seen it for myself, but isolation... isolation sounds good."

"That sounds nice," I said.

I sat in the break room. Bone was dead asleep on a table holding a beer. I sat on the couch, staring at the screen on the wall. My eyes were getting heavy. I could feel sleep clawing its way into my brain. I was jolted a little by Shades sitting next to me. He had a large grin slapped across his face.

"Sleepy, huh?" he asked.

I didn't respond.

"You're a real talker, y'know that?"

Nothing.

"You and Tab were out pretty late. Pretty tough job, huh?"

"You can say that," I said.

"Woah! It speaks! I was gonna call medical, thought you were having a stroke."

I stood up from the couch.

"Oh c'mon," said Shades. "One joke at your expense and you're gonna leave?"

I craned my neck towards him. Shades pointed his finger at me and shook it up and down.

"That face," he said. "Disobedient and disapproving? Tsk, tsk. Those looks aren't gonna get you far."

"I'm sorry," I said. "Why are you here?"

"Why am I here? C'mon, man. You just keep pushing back, even if you don't know it."

"I'm sorry?"

"Look, we're in a bad situation, right?"

"Right."

"Then, why take the path of most resistance? We can work with them instead of against them."

"They're extorting us."

"Maybe they are, but what're you gonna do about it?"

I walked away from the conversation at that point. I didn't know what Shades was getting at there, but he'll be stuck here while Tab and I will be free.

* * *

I found my way to a bedroom the company had made for me. It was minimalist in every way possible. Cream walls, white bed sheets, and not even a desk. There was only a small dresser and shower in the room.

I laid back on the bed and started up at the ceiling. My arm itched and I scratched it unintentionally. I looked over to make sure I didn't ruin the synthetic skin. It was fine, just a little red and sore.

I dug through the dresser to see if there was anything in it. Nothing. Not even clothes. The only thing you could do in here was shower and sleep.

I decided to shower first. The suds sat in my hair as I stared down the drain. There was nothing about the room that made me comfortable. It felt like I couldn't do anything without something over my shoulder.

I got out of the shower as soon as I could and laid down on the bed in my jeans and shirt. I stared at the cream-colored ceiling again. It made me think about what these people want from us. They want the people they've taken from to be unnoticed like a cream-colored wall. They expect us to be expectable, and fade into the paint they put on the wall.

That thought filled me with rage in my head and heat in my hands. I grabbed my bat and held it up. I wanted to swing at the wall. I should have. Instead, I put it down and sat down on the bed. My head held low, looking at the tile floor.

I couldn't just let this happen, but how could I fight back? It felt like an impossible question to find an answer to.

I let the thought die as I laid back on the mattress, and tried to get some sleep.

I rode in the passenger seat of Tab's car. She nudged me on the arm.

"You get any sleep?" she asked. "You seem a little out of it today."

"No, I've just been thinking," I said.

"Thinking? That's dangerous stuff."

I rolled my head over to her and gave her an annoyed look.

"I'm kidding!" she said. "What's on your mind?"

"It's nothing."

"Alright, Mister Secret Agent. I'll try to keep it quick today then, alright? Let's just do this job and make sure you can use that EMP right."

She looked at her forearm and tapped it twice. Text appeared on her arm.

"We're after a guy who owes the company an eye," she said. "Let's try to wrap this up."

We drove until we made it into a run-down part of the city. The screens on some buildings were glitching in and out. A lot of the buildings were in complete ruin. I saw a lot of people with mods that didn't seem to match their bodies at all. I saw a young boy with a right arm that was red and far larger than his left arm.

"They're Modjunkies," said Tab. "They first get a mod to protect themselves if their house gets robbed, then they keep doing it until their bodies need it."

"They need their mods?" I asked.

"A lot of them do, their muscle structure would probably give out without them."

"You think our target is a Modjunky?"

"Maybe. Just keep an eye out."

We drove down more and more streets. Some of the people looked at us driving by, while others minded their own business. I saw a woman holding an infant. The infant had a swollen lump on its chest and a tub connecting that lump to its shoulder. I turned my head away. I couldn't look anymore.

We stopped on the side of the road in front of a shabby two-story house. A large piece of the roof was missing on its left side, it looked like something blew it off with an explosion.

Tab checked her arm, then checked the address of the house. She opened the door and walked out.

"This is the place," she said.

I got out of the car.

"Keep your cool," she said. "We got this one job, then we're out of here."

We walked to the door. Tab knocked. There wasn't a response. She knocked again.

"Anybody home?" she asked.

The door unlocked and creaked open just enough for us to see a face. A woman stood in the doorway in front of us.

"What do you want?" she asked.

"Randy here?" Tab replied.

"Who?"

"Randy. Skinny white guy? Blue eyes?"

"I don't know a Randy."

"Well, this is his house."

I leaned back while Tab argued with the woman. I saw a face peek at me from behind the window to my right. It was a face pale with blue eyes. I looked startled and closed the curtains in a panic.

While the woman continued to argue with Tab, I kicked the door open. The woman was thrown back a few feet. I pulled out my bat and ran into the house. I saw Randy run upstairs.

"I GOT HIM!" I yelled.

The woman got off the floor. She elongated her arm, wrapped it around my leg, and yanked back. I fell to the floor. The woman grew needles out of the fingers on her free hand.

"GO UPSTAIRS AND HE DIES!" she yelled. "I MEAN IT! I'LL KILL THE BASTARD!"

"Alright," Tab said. "Ghost, keep your head down."

I threw my hands over my head and threw my head to the floor. Tab yanked a submachine gun and unloaded it onto the woman. All I heard was *GAK GAK*

GAK GAK and then the woman fell to the floor. I looked over and saw the woman's body on the ground covered in bullet holes with brown-yellow oil leaking out of them.

Tab grabbed my hand and lifted me off the floor.

"Let's get him," said Tab.

I ran upstairs before she did. I took a moment to look around before I saw Randy curled up in the bathroom.

I walked into the bathroom. I leaned over him. Randy curled into himself.

"I NEED IT!" he yelled. "MORE THAN YOU!"

He uncurled and his back slapped against the wall.

"Y'know," he shook. "I feel bad for you. Y'know, you Reapers. I know who I am, but you Reapers, you don't know a single thing about yourselves. You don't know why you're doing this, doing that, why you have names, nothing. You're like babies with guns."

I held out my bat, he pushed himself further onto the wall. He spread out like goo hitting a hard surface.

"C'mon man," he jittered. "You don't gotta get violent."

"Ghost," said Tab. "Just get the eye already."

I leaned over Randy, his eyes locked with mine.

"I need you to hand me over the eye you stole," I said.

"You mean. . . this one?"

He slapped the back of his head, and his left eye rolled out and landed in the palm of his hand. It started to tick. The pupil flashed red.

"KABOOM!" he laughed.

178

The ticking got quicker.

"GET THE HELL OUT OF THERE!" yelled Tab.

We needed this eye. I flexed my arm and a wave of static emanated from my body. I rolled over Randy, and I'm pretty sure it went out of the bathroom. The eye stopped ticking. Randy craned his head up at me, his face read of confusion and terror.

"Was that an—"

I crashed my bat into the top of his head. He smashed into the wall and flopped unconscious in the bathtub. Tab stepped in behind me.

"Make sure to double-tap," she said.

"What?"

"Hit him on the head, just to make sure."

I swung again.

* * *

We were back in a spot that was becoming a new home to me, Tab's car. She grinned at me.

"You did great back there," she said. "I didn't think you'd whip out the EMP like that. I thought it'd take a while for you to figure out how to use it."

"I don't know," I said. "I just saw what you did with your arm, and just. . . did it."

"Huh. You catch on quick."

"I guess so."

"Well, you know what that means for us?"

I shrugged.

"It means. . . we can probably get outta here quicker."

"Really?"

"Yeah, really."

Tab parked us in an alleyway. She looked around for a few moments to make sure we were clear.

"So. . . here's the plan," she said.

"Alright," I said.

"We're gonna meet up in the break room tomorrow, and before we go out on a job, I want you to blast that EMP as hard as you can."

"What? I just used it once. You think I can—"

"Look, I don't know where but they probably have some security response system. If we get a job, they'll probably have some kind of program to let us out. If we can get it to somehow. . . lock in that state, we can ride as far as possible."

"Alright. What about the guards?"

"Why do you think I have so many guns? Do you think it was for jobs? These people are nobodies, they can barely defend themselves from a cold."

Tab leaned over and grabbed her bag.

"Do you want one before we start tomorrow?"

"Uh. . ."

"Don't be a baby. You're getting a gun."

She placed a handgun spray-painted red in my lap.

"Are you scared of it?" she asked.

"No."

"Good. You'll need it."

* * *

I was jittery as hell. I kept tapping the area of my pants where I kept my gun hidden. I stayed in my room for a little too long that morning. My foot tapped against the tile floor. I waited for Tab to knock on my door to let me know the plan was still happening, but it never came.

After a moment of reassuring myself, I left my room and made my way to the break room. The break room was darker than usual. The lights were off, the screen was off, and not even Bone was in there in a drunken sleep. The only sound I heard was a *CHIK CHIK* and a light orange glow of a cigarette.

The figure smoking stood up and snapped their fingers. The lights flashed on, I was almost blinded. There stood Shades, smoking a cigarette.

"So," he said. "It's come to this, huh?"

"The hell are you talking about?" I asked.

"Right, right. You wouldn't know would you?"

I stared him down.

"There's that look again. Guess you're just naturally insubordinate, aren't you, Ghost?"

"Where's Tab?"

"I wouldn't worry about her at the moment, let's set everything right, shall we?"

I drew out my gun and aimed it right at his head.

"Jesus Christ," groaned Shades. "You don't know when you've lost."

"Take a step and I plant one in your head."

"That's a new one, new loop?"

"What?"

"Oh c'mon, you aren't getting a sense that you've

done all this before? Y'know. Fighting a losing battle?"

Shades made one step toward me. I fired. Before the bullet landed, it crashed into a cyan pentagon and bounced on the floor. The pentagon faded away.

"I'll give you a bit of an explanation," said Shades. "Just for fun."

Shades took off his pair of navy blue sunglasses. His form changed, it looked like a digital glitch surrounded his body before it morphed into its real look. In his place, stood a man wearing a business suit with a purple tie. He put on a new pair of purple sunglasses with rounded lenses.

"Mashima?"

"I'm surprised none of you caught on," he said. "The disguise was obvious. I didn't even try to hide it."

"You've been. . . keeping an eye on us the whole time."

"Yes, I have been."

A fire grew in my mind and my body. My hands shook, I aimed once more and fired. The bullet bounced off another pentagon that quickly fades away.

"What do you plan to accomplish here?"

"I. . . I'm freeing myself."

"FREE?" Mashima gave a bellowing laugh. "Of course, that's what this is all about, isn't it?"

He approached me, and I fired four more shots. They all bounced off his shield. Once close enough, he right-hooked me so hard that I crashed into the coffee table and broke it. He yanked me up by the collar, took his sunglasses off, and locked eyes with me.

"Let me explain something, Ghost. I gave you, I gave *ALL OF YOU* so many chances! I wanted to reintegrate you into something better! Before you were nothing. YOU WERE SHIT BENEATH THE WORLD'S BOOT! But I gave you your shot! I'M YOUR PATRON SAINT! But who gets crucified? ME!"

He threw me into the wall.

"Use that EMP," he growled. "You want your chance? Use that EMP."

I looked at my arm and then back at him.

"Use. It."

I held out my gun and aimed it at him. He dashed and kicked it out of my hand. It skidded into the bathroom.

"USE IT!" he yelled.

I put so much pressure on my arm. I charged that EMP like it was the last thing I was ever going to do. It burned against my skin, the synthetic skin melted and bubbled against the heat of the implant. I locked eyes with Mashima.

"Go ahead," he said. "Fire."

I let it all go. It sounded like an explosion ripped through my arm and into the rest of the building. At that moment, my head felt something fill it. A sense of familiarity. I saw images of a family, a brother, and my first car. But something was off, I saw memories overlapping each other like film scenes playing over one another. I saw a memory where I was part of a punk crew, another where I was a nurse, and so many others. I couldn't grasp what was real and what wasn't.

I stood there heaving air in and out, eyes locked with Mashima. Rage boiled through my veins, laughter exploded from my mouth, and tears ran down my cheeks.

Mashima pointed at me.

"That's it," he said. "Let it all in."

I went to grab his throat. Mashima swung a left hook into my neck. I took the hit and got my right hand on his throat and squeezed. Mashima took his elbow to my right temple. I stumbled and fell to my knees. He kicked me in the stomach. He started to yell about something as he kept stomping down on my back. My vision was getting hazy, and I fell unconscious.

* * *

I felt like I was drifting along an airy river in darkness. A heat would pass through parts of my body, but it was strongest in my head. I could feel everything being burnt away, but I didn't know what exactly was burnt away. Images and sounds that barely meant anything to me, all up in smoke.

Ever had your mind screwed with? It's not a good feeling. To be honest, I'm still trying to grasp what exactly I lost.

* * *

Noah Browning is many things: a writer, Film-maker, an Overthinker, and an overall creative. Heavily influenced by various science fiction and fantasy authors such as Douglas Adams, Neal Stephenson, Terry Pratchett, and Michael Crichton. He is Florida-born but raised by New Jersey natives, thus he grew up with an interesting clashing of cultures and values. Born Physically disabled, he spent most of his time interacting with various forms of artistic media. Growing up with an overdeveloped sense of media literacy, he strives to one day make his impact with a piece of his own.

Hávamál

by Deborah
Sale-Butler

Hávamál

By Deborah Sale-Butler

As I hang impaled on a tentacle of the hideous octopus bannister Robert bought me for my fortieth birthday, I have thoughts about my life decisions.

Starting with the octopus. It was hate at first sight. Robert had the thing installed while I was in Boston, running my third marathon. I walked into the foyer to find it dominated by a four-foot-high, twenty-five-foot-long, distressed pewter sculpture, whose tentacles twisted, twirled and stretched to form a bannister on our curved marble staircase.

Most of its limbs anchored a glowering head to the stairs and formed the hand-rail, but two tentacles rose dramatically above the evil face, forming what looked like an enormous handlebar mustache.

"Isn't it great? I know how much you like octo-pusses and I just couldn't resist!"

I had never shown any interest in octopi. Ever. And now I had a steampunk horror-show sauropod looming over my entryway. As usual, I kept my disappointment to myself. After all, Robert seemed so pleased with his thoughtful gift. There were few moments of him being pleased with anything lately.

The irony of my painful, impending demise is that I lost my balance looking at an image on my phone— a picture of a woman wearing an octopus necklace (and nothing else) with her arm around my husband. I knew three things in an instant: he bought the sculpture to impress her, he'd probably already brought her to the house, and the accidental selfie/text was no accident.

She wanted me to know.

I had just gotten out of bed and in that moment of shock—I lost track of myself in space, took one step off the second-floor landing and tumbled into the arms of the waiting beast. The phone landed on the step beside me, mocking me with the picture of Robert on his "work trip" to Chicago.

The octopus skewered me through the shoulder, blood pooling under the foot that I was using to push up and try to keep myself from settling deeper onto the pointy tentacle. My other foot could almost reach the phone. I stretched my left leg as far as I could and touched the phone with my big toe. Each reach tore deeper into my right shoulder. I dissolved into helpless tears.

A stanza of an old Norse poem came to me on the next wave of pain:

Wounded I hung on a windswept tree
nine long nights,
run through with a spear, dedicated to Odin,
myself to myself

I could hear David reading his translation to me over a bottle of cheap red wine in the dingy room he shared, just off campus, with four other students.

I scolded him, "But it *literally* says '*I know* I hung on a windswept tree'!"

"Yes, but the alliteration carries the line better, "wounded" connects him to "windswept tree" and to his pain."

I could listen to him talk about poetry in his soft British accent for hours and never tire of it. And I couldn't resist kissing him when his lips rounded to form the repeating W's.

"Rhythm, language, history—It's all connected," he'd said, pressing his fingertips to mine. "We've carried the stories inside us as long as we have walked the Earth—the sounds and beats of the poetry, like a living heart." He placed his hand on my heart and I felt the connection—to him, to a broader world, to new possibilities in myself.

He asked me to join him in London after graduation. Dad caught me on my way to the airport. "I did not pay for four years of college for you to fuck off to England with a goddamned poet. Do you ever think of how the things you do affect anyone else? Do you?"

I held a nonrefundable ticket and a suitcase in my hands. All I needed to do was walk out the door and hail a cab. But right behind dad, I could see my mother's pleading eyes. I carried my bag back up to my room. At the time, I thought my mother was begging me to stay.

Another shock of pain carries the realization that my mother had wanted me to call that cab.

Stanzas of Hávamál echo in my head in David's lovely voice:

downwards I peered;

I took up the runes, screaming I took them,

then I fell back from there.

Take up those goddamn runes. I know I can't pick up the phone. But I can call on deus ex machina.

"Siri!"

"Yes, Carla?"

"Call 911."

Then I began to quicken and be wise,

and to grow and to prosper;

The ambulance is on its way.

one word from another word found a word for me,

I want to say "thanks" to the woman I've never met.

one deed from another deed found a deed for me...

You stabbed me in the heart, but I will thrive. I'll save the text and sue for divorce (before you do, darling Robert).

After I heal, I think I'll take a trip to England and check up on an old friend.

* * *

Deborah Sale-Butler is a Portland Oregon based writer whose articles and short stories have appeared in the "Dead Girls Walking" anthology, and many online magazines including "Commuter Lit," "Flash Fiction Magazine," "Still Point Arts Quarterly," and "Underside Stories." You can find links to her work at https://deborah-sale-butler.com

About the Authors

Dear Authors of Three x the Fun,

You are the coolest, chillest bunch of authors we've ever worked with! Thank you for trusting us with your work.

Love, Rebellion LIT

* * *

The talented authors featured in Three x the Fun reminded us of what being an author is like. Creativity, freedom, and inside stories making it to the outside.

Be sure to mention your favorite stories in your review.

Also From Rebellion LIT

Kisses in the Dark by Marlowe Westley Pulliam

Elevated Inferno by Carlotta Ardell

Breaking Point by Carlotta Ardell

Helpless: A short story collection by Tiffany Christina Lewis

Alyssa Fairfield by Tiffany Christina Lewis

The Michael Taylor Series

The Start: First Annual Anthology

Two for the Show: Second Annual Anthology